JACKIE VERONA
The Devil's Music

A DIGEST NOVEL BY
KIMBERLY B. RICHARDSON

Acknowledgments:

To ProSe Productions - thank you, as always.

To my friends - thank you for being you.

I HUGGED HIM as tightly as I possibly could. He, thankfully, didn't cry out in pain but only hugged me even tighter. I still couldn't believe that my friend, the world renowned sax player Philippe Vervain, was actually sitting across from me on my couch. I knew that tears were in my eyes but I didn't care. I finally released him, yet we continued to hold hands.

"Jackie," Philippe said in his deep tone with a hint of French that I adored, "thanks for having me here."

"Thank Clovis," I replied with a warm smile. "He was the one who finally booked your trio. Took three long years but damn it, it's worth it."

He leaned back in the couch and pulled out a pack of cigarettes followed by a lighter, giving me more than enough of a reason to pull out my pack from my purse. He lit his, then leaned forward to light mine. He snapped the lighter shut with a flair that only he possessed.

"Gaulois, I assume," I said with a smirk as I stared at the small blue box.

"*Mais oui, cher*," he replied with a wink. "It's the French in me, ya know." Philippe Vervain was one of those friends in which you could go for weeks or months or even years not hearing from him, only to receive a letter or phone call and the friendship would pick up where it left off with no bumps. Ever since he made it big with his first album titled New Orleans in the Rain, he'd been on the road, promoting his trio called The Fleur de Lis Trio. All three of the members were from New Orleans.

"Do you remember when my mom made you that cake?" I asked after blowing a stream of smoke into the air. "The one with the nuts?"

"Ahhh, yeah, I also remember eating half of it in one sitting," Philippe replied after taking a long drag off his cigarette. "Made me so sick but it was worth it. By the way, how are they doing? Give them my love next time."

"They're fine and still fighting the good fight," I replied after taking a sip of my tea. "It won't end until there is equality between coloreds and whites." Philippe nodded sagely and then finished off his cigarette by crushing it in my ashtray. If you merely glanced at Philippe, you would think - white man - and be on your way. However, if you stopped to actually take in a good look, you would find that there was much, much more. For starters, he was from a very old and wealthy Creole family,with a good blend of French, African, Native American, and even some Italian thrown in for good measure. All of that resulted in his family having beautiful light olive skin, and jet black hair with the slightest curl to it. However, Philippe had bright blue eyes, making every woman who saw him immediately go coo-coo for him. To the world, he was a handsome white man. To me, he was one of my dearest friends.

"I've never understood that tea thing," he said with a now exaggerated French accent that always made me laugh. He winked as he picked up his cup of strong black coffee and took a long sip. "Ahh," he said with a sigh as he set the cup on my table, "why drink lukewarm colored water when you can have the gift of coffee?"

"Phil," I said with a smirk (he hated being called Phil yet was only mildly annoyed when I said it), "you'll never get me to drink that stuff. Too rough on my delicate nature." That caused him to laugh.

Just then, someone knocked on my door. I got up and walked toward it, thinking it was my wonderful husband, Clovis, yet when I opened the door, I was pleasantly surprised.

"Normally I would have called, but where's the fun in that?" My best friend and partner in crime Monica, or Mooney, strolled in with her usual grace and poise. She wore black pants and a white top, while her long red hair was piled up on top of her head, making her look like a Roman goddess. She looked around, saw Philippe, and then cried out, "Oh my god!" She raced over to the couch and immediately pulled out her camera, ready to take several shots of my friend. Philippe raised his eyebrows in surprise and somewhat leaned back.

"I guess I don't need to introduce you two?" I said as I returned to Philippe and sat in the chair across from them.

"You might need to tell me who *she* is and why she's taking photos of me," Philippe replied as he tried to relax while Mooney clicked on.

"My friend Monica, world class photographer and world traveler," I said by way of introduction.

"And you're the amazing Philippe Vervain of the Fleur de Lis Trio," Mooney finished as she took two more shots, then lowered her camera as she extended her hand out. "It truly is a pleasure meeting you. I have all of your albums and I understand you'll be performing later this week?" Philippe, now relieved that she wasn't some crazy person, shook her hand. Before I could ask her how she knew so much in so little time, she turned to me and said, "You know that nothing's a secret to me."

"You get around," I said with a laugh. "Want any tea?"

"I'm good," she replied with a raised hand. "Just wanted

to drop in and see if I was right about him being here." She gave him one long look and said, "Guess I was." She then got up from the couch with the same manner of grace she had with everything else and let herself out. Philippe watched her leave while I cleaned out the ashtray. I knew the questions would be coming soon. As soon as I heard the door close from the kitchen, I walked out with a clean ashtray to find Philippe lighting another cigarette. He narrowed his eyes at me, as though I'd willingly held back a secret from him.

"*Cher*," he said in a thoughtful tone, "who was that goddess? I admit that she scared me when she pulled out her camera, yet I have to know more about that divine creature whom you call friend." He took a long drag off his Gaulois and blew a thick stream of smoke that passed by my face by inches. I coughed a little.

"Yes, she really is a world class photographer and artist and lover of the arts," I started, "plus, she's a patron of the arts as well. Wealthy as hell and yet one of the cheapest people I've ever known." I reached for my pack of smokes for what I was about to say next - how would he take it, I wondered. By the look in his eyes, I had to say it. That poor New Orleans man was about to fall in love with one of the most unavailable women in Moon City. "Um... Philippe," I said as I pulled out a cigarette, which he quickly lit and then took another drag from his, "I really hate to tell you this, but seeing as how you're . . . well, um anyway, Monica is a lesbian." You could have heard a pin drop in the entire city. He began to choke, causing his cigarette to fall to the floor. I screamed as I quickly dove for it and then stamped it out in the ashtray. There was no damage to my floor or anything else. I breathed a sigh of relief. Philippe didn't seem to notice. He was still in shock.

"Lesbian? Her? That goddess with the red hair?" He jumped up and started to pace behind the couch.

So dramatic, I thought with a sad smile. "Weren't you thinking she was a psycho or something only minutes before?"

"Yeah but her looks . . . *Mon dieu!*" He made the sign of the cross and I shook my head.

"Jeez, it's not the end of the world, ya know. I'm sure you're got more than one girl on your arm no matter where you are," I finished and then enjoyed my cigarette in peace. Philippe continued his shock, of course.

"B-but, Jackie! And by the way, I'm not a player. Not when it comes to women. I don't like that whole facade of the jazz player who can't get enough. No," he said as he sat down once more to reach for another cigarette and lit it, "I'm a one woman kind of man. It means more to me, no?" He shook his head as his latest cigarette balanced delicately on his bottom lip. "Sorry about dropping, it," he added and then sighed. "Lesbian?"

"Lesbian. But hey, you've impressed her, being who you are. If anything, you've made a good friend." I leaned in closer as though I had a secret to tell him. "Which by the way . . . are you seeing anyone?"

"If I was," Philippe said as he sat up straight with pride, "I wouldn't have gone goo goo for your friend. Alas, I am alone. All I have is my music. And my books of course. And my strong coffee that tastes nothing like your thin tea water!"

I merely sighed. *It sure was great seeing Philippe again*, I thought to myself. The good and the bad, all rolled into one really flaky croissant. "Oh yeah," Philippe added, "Clovis told me about that murder you solved." He shivered. "Gruesome, man."

I nodded sagely as memories from the previous year

came rushing back. *Had it been a year since I buried my friend Dianne and discovered who had killed her?* I nodded to myself as Philippe went silent.

"Clovis can finally talk about it," I said. "The tears don't come as frequent now. He can actually smile whenever he mentions her or I do."

"Some crazy woman, right?"

"Yeah, the sister of this dude Dianne was seeing. He kept saying that he was innocent and I believed him. He was an asshole but a killer? Nah. His sister, however, was more than capable of committing several murders. What a piece of work. She even hit on me once. Thank god Monica was there."

"Whatever happened to her?"

"Sent to an asylum and then later found dead amid some flowers. I still think she killed herself, but Clovis thought that another patient may have killed her." I shrugged as I finished off my cigarette; being around Philippe made me smoke more than normal. I took a sip of my very cold tea and said, "That was a strange time. Oh yeah," I said with a sly look, "Monica assisted me with figuring out the killer."

"Ahh, of course she did," Philippe sighed. "Pure beauty with brains. Of course, you've never had stupid people in your life, as far as I can remember." I had to agree with that. I couldn't tolerate stupidity. My mind thought about Officer Held and how, at first, he was so odd towards me during the time of that investigation. Later, I learned that he wasn't used to educated colored people like me. *What a shame. I wonder how he would feel in meeting a fellow New Orleanian like Philippe?* Speaking of which, I continued to think since it seemed that Philippe was done with talking for a while, I hadn't spoken with either Hancock or Held since my wedding. I knew that Hancock was still involved with Jane, the owner of the cafe I always visit, yet I hadn't seen him whenever I was there. Every time I asked about him, Jane would smile in that dreamy way and say that he was fine. I didn't want to know the details about that. However, the last time I was there, she told me that he was still working on that child kidnapping case with no strong leads. Although I was pleased to solve Dianne's murder, as gruesome as it was, I vowed that I really didn't want to ever do that again. I wanted my life of writing, jazz music, drinking tea, and smoking to fill it. No more murders, please.

—⚜—

CLOVIS FINALLY SHOWED up an hour later, to which I was somewhat relieved. After telling him about last year's murder, Philippe returned to talking about Monica and if she'd ever been with a man. I answered him that she liked what she liked and that was that. So, he tried asking me the same question in different ways. And, every time I replied with the same answer. When Clovis showed up, I literally fell back into my chair.

"Hey hey, there's the man himself!" The two jumped up and gave each other a hearty handshake. "My wonderful other half keeping you entertained?"

"Ah yeah, but I'm sad - she told me about Monica." I rolled my eyes while Clovis laughed.

"Man, there are plenty of other women out there." He walked over to me and pulled me into an embrace. "Plenty of Jackies out there." He kissed my cheek and I wanted to melt into that kiss, yet held myself back. Clovis was the only man who truly understood me. We were both artists, albeit in different forms, and our vibes just got on well with each other. It was damn near perfect. Even though he was white and I was coloured, our love surpassed the colour of our skin. I also knew that he would never be the same after burying his little sister. "But enough of that," he said as he pulled away from me, "you and your guys ready for tonight? I know it'll be a packed house. Everyone in Moon City knows about the Fleur de Lis Trio!"

" I'm just glad we're here," Philippe replied with a warm smile. "Besides, it gives me time to play catch up with Jackie. It's been too long." He checked his watch and sighed. "And now, I've got to say *au bientot*. Gotta meet up with my guys to go over some notes." He kissed me on the cheek, gave one more handshake to Clovis, and then left with a jaunty wave of his hand. I locked the door behind him and started cleaning up.

"How long have you known each other?" Clovis asked as he helped me with the cups as I walked into the kitchen.

"Apparently, we first met when we were kids, but I don't remember much. I'd say, oh I don't know, a long ass time!" Clovis laughed as he set the cups in the sink.

"Get to writing, little lady," he said as he slapped a dish towel over his shoulder. "I'll take care of everything else." I nodded my thanks and returned to my writing studio. I closed the door behind me, sat in my comfortable and well worn chair, and then took a good look at my typewriter. I raised my hands up like a conductor, only to lower them into my lap. *One year*, I thought. *One year ago, our lives changed.* I raised my hands again and slowly began to type. *Another year, another book,* I thought. I stopped again as Dianne's face came into focus. Bright kid with so much promise, only to be killed by a crazy jealous woman.

—ᴍ—

LATER THAT DAY, Mooney returned to our house to prepare for tonight's concert. Clovis left an hour after coming home, leaving me to write in peace. Yet, after my conversation with Philippe, my mind was anything but. I buckled down on myself and typed anything that came out of me. At first, I typed only nonsense and vents of frustration until the groove finally kicked in and I was back on track. I typed for three hours straight and then got up to take a stretch break, only to stop when someone knocked on my door. I made my way to the door and opened it, revealing a grinning Mooney with clothes bags draped over one arm.

"I have to get my outfit perfect for tonight," she said as she walked in, gave me a quick kiss on the cheek, and then sauntered to our bedroom to unload her wares.

"In all of my time knowing you," I said as I leaned against the door frame, "you've never looked less than perfect."

"You're just sayin' that," Mooney replied as she started to unzip her bags and pull out several dresses. "Hmmm," she murmured as she tapped a manicured fingernail against her chin, "does tonight call for pants or a dress? Decisions!" She whirled around to face me with an accusing stare. "And what are *you* wearing tonight?" she asked as she crossed her arms over her chest.

"Something black and simple," I replied with a shrug.

"Oh yeah, you've broken my friend's heart." Mooney dropped her accusing stance and replaced it with a confused one.

"Huh?"

"My friend, Philippe," I informed her. "He's heartbroken that you aren't into men. He couldn't stop talking about you with that crazy French accent of his."

"Yeah," Mooney replied with a little dreamy look in her eye, "I *did* like the French accent. But, he's a boy and no thanks." She sat on the edge of my bed and crossed her legs. I sighed inwardly; everything she did was perfect. I didn't think there was such a thing as a perfect human, but Mooney was it. "So," she added as her eyes narrowed in mischievous glee, "how much did he talk about me?"

"Good lord, don't go on breaking his heart," I replied as I joined her on the bed and began looking through her outfits. "He was serious, though. He liked you."

"Can't be helped, Jackie." She got up and proceeded to open a small bag filled with earrings. She poured the contents on the bed and ran her hand through them. "What's it like being married?" she asked out of the blue. I raised my face toward hers and noticed something strange in her eyes. Was she . . .

"It's been swell," I replied as I pulled up a slinky black dress, then got up to hold it against me. "Divine. Anyway, Clovis and I work really well together."

"Do you miss your apartment? The freedom?"

"Well, I still have my freedom, thanks to my writing and his music sessions." I looked at her again and then realized what it was - "Hey," I said as I set the dress on the bed, "are you okay?"

She shrugged, "Sure. Never been better."

"You're a terrible liar," I sighed as I got up and went into the kitchen. I returned to the bedroom ten minutes later with two cups of oolong tea to find her wiping her eyes while surrounded by her dresses. She looked like a strange and sad peacock. I handed her one of the cups and then sat next to her.

"I'm not a liar," Mooney murmured as she wiped her face

again, "but . . .well, Jackie, I envy you. You're got this special man in your life, your writing is flourishing, and you seem to be so laid back and cool about it."

"Coming from the Goddess of Glamour," I smirked, then took a sip of tea.

"I . . . can't show my affection outside like you can," Mooney said with a straight face. She blew on her tea and then took a tiny sip.

"You think it's any easier for me?" I scoffed. "I'm a colored woman married to a white man! There are laws that make my marriage illegal. There are people right now who would kill Clovis and rape me." I leaned toward her and placed a hand on top of hers. "You're white. I'm not. I love you dearly, Mooney, but to the outside world, I am beneath you."

"And that's such bullshit!" Mooney took a larger sip of her tea. "Jackie, ever since I first met you, I knew you and I would hit it off. Ever since then and even when you learned that I was a lesbian, you've been right by my side."

I perked up. "Hey, has anyone -"

She raised up a hand to silence me. "Not recently, but you know how it goes. Don't let some man see you walk into *those* kinds of clubs. Thank goodness I haven't run across one who waited for me outside, ready to bash my head in or something just as gruesome." She stared at her tea thoughtfully. "I want your kind of stability, Jackie." I was shocked; here was one of the top photographers and artists and patrons ever, and she envied me? I shook my head and took another sip of my cooling tea.

"Monica," I said in a low tone, "drink your tea and then I'll help you figure out what to wear tonight. Be yourself, okay? Your wild and amazing self." Monica looked as though she was about to cry again, only to return to her former grinning self. She finished off her tea and then jumped up to begin trying on her outfits with me as her sole audience. As she tried on each outfit with flair, my mind thought about our earlier conversation. Thankfully, I hadn't had too many encounters regarding my race in Moon City, yet they were still there. They still happened to me. Never mind the fact that I was a highly educated colored woman with several published books. I was still a coloured woman.

Thirty minutes later, Mooney finally decided on one of her more revealing indigo coloured dresses that left nothing to the imagination.

"Well," she asked as she twirled around in her dress, "what d'ya think?" She twirled once more, then bowed before me. I clapped my approval and she hugged me as a reply. "This'll knock the socks off everyone," she said as she removed her dress and returned to her former wear.

"You just love teasing men, don't you?" I replied as I assisted her in getting everything back into their proper bags.

"Nonsense," she replied but I knew she was lying. "I just like looking my best and if it happens to drive some people crazy, well…" She left her thoughts trail off as she scooped up her jewelry and returned it to its bag. "Besides, I may meet the woman of my dreams tonight!" Mooney noticed that I was quiet so she asked, "Hey, does my talk of other women bother you sometimes?" I looked up at her in slight shock. "'Cause if it does, I can stop, ya know? You're one of my best friends."

"And you know damn well that you don't need to worry about me and how I feel about you," I replied, then grabbed her arms and stared right into her eyes. "Monica, you are one of my best friends as well. Not to mention one hell of a sidekick when it comes to solving crazy murders." She grinned at that. "I don't care who you sleep with or think is cute, okay?" I shook her lightly once for emphasis, but I think she got the point. I released her arms, only to almost be knocked over by her hugging me.

"Remember when we spent the night in jail?" she said while laughing.

"How could I ever forget that?"

She pulled away from me. "I wouldn't want anyone else with me in that situation but you. Besides, who else would I have taken to my special club?"

"Ah yeah. The Mai Tais and Althea gettin' fresh with me." Mooney shivered, causing me to laugh. "Okay, can we stop with the sentimental crap and get ready for tonight?"

Mooney laughed. "No problem but now I want a cig. Join me?" We left my bedroom and returned to the living room for a much needed cigarette break. We sat on the couch and both lit at the same time. Mooney sighed as she exhaled a stream of smoke. "Full club tonight?"

"Oh yeah," I replied, sinking deeper into the couch. "Fleur de Lis' first time performing in Moon City. Everyone who is everyone will be there tonight." I knew that Clovis was beside himself in getting the infamous jazz trio to perform here for one night. Lots of pulled strings and probably bribes, knowing my lovely husband. I took another drag off my cigarette and exhaled slowly: so far, my life was going pretty good. I glanced at Monica, who had pulled out a candy bar from her purse. She offered it to me but I declined.

A S THE LAST rays of sun disappeared, giving way to the night, Monica and I were on our way to the club to watch Fleur de Lis perform their hearts out in the name of jazz. We took Mooney's car, of course - we had to arrive in style. As we pulled up to the front door, a well dressed valet immediately appeared by my door and helped me out of the car, then rushed over to help Mooney.

"Get your hands off me," she said in a playful tone as she swatted his gloved hands away. "I appreciate the gesture but no." She then handed the keys to him and then linked arms with me as we strolled inside. As soon as we crossed the threshold, Angel, the owner of the club, came waltzing up to us with a million dollar watt grin plastered on his face, while his body was encased in a black suit that actually fit him well. He grabbed our hands and kissed them repeatedly.

"Monica, baby, Jackie baby!" he yelled as he continued to kiss our hands, then pulled back to admire us both. "Lovely ladies for a lovely night!" He weaved his arms around in excitement. "The place is packed and we're still takin' in folks! You two, of course, sit up front!" Before we could reply, he grabbed our hands and led us through the throng of people toward the stage. He pulled out the chairs for us and then helped us sit down, then floated off to help other patrons to their seats. I knew Clovis was backstage helping out, yet I wanted to see my man. I told Mooney I'd be back and then made my way behind the black curtains. I located Clovis, dressed in a spectacular black suit, talking with Philippe and the other members of the trio; he looked up, saw me, and then raced toward me and enveloped me in a hug.

"Delight, you look yummy!" he said as he nearly tried to crush me. I laughed while pushing him away, then smoothed out my dress. Following Mooney's direction, I decided to throw on a slinky little black number and wear my single strand of pearls around my neck. Hair piled high and well done (thanks to Mooney), plus red lipstick and a hint of cologne behind each pearl earring dangling ear. My black framed cat glasses completed the look and apparently it was quite a look. Clovis couldn't stop staring at me, along with several other men who gave me appreciative looks and whistles.

"Alright now," Clovis said as he snaked an arm around my waist, "this one's mine! Go get your own!" He kissed my cheek and then added, "You and Mooney tonight?"

"Oh yeah. Front table and everything."

"I told Angel to do that. Naturally, he agreed." He kissed me again, longer this time, as he whispered, "Can't wait to get you home, Delight." I wanted to melt into his arms and tell him that I loved him until the end of time. Instead, I gently pried away from him and then walked toward Philippe, whose eyes were focused on me but more of a brotherly way.

"*Mon cher*," he said with a grin, "you look *fantastique!*" He kissed my hand and then said, "Jackie, meet the members of Fleur de Lis - Jean, our drummer, and Leon, our bassist." Both men nodded their heads at me and I gave them a smile they wouldn't forget. Jean was tall and lanky with skin the colour of a chocolate bar. His face, complete with soul patch, looked too young to be 40, while his hazel eyes seemed to sparkle. Leon was a white man my height with muscular arms and a full beard. Horn rimmed glasses framed his long face with narrow nose and crystal blue eyes. I think the boy was blushing as I smiled at him.

"Good luck tonight but you don't need it," I told the trio. "You guys are legends in the jazz world." I then waved goodbye and returned to Mooney. As I approached the table, I noticed that she had ordered drinks for us. I sat down next to her and raised my glass of chilled vodka as a toast.

Although the club was packed with anticipating and excited people, the level of noise was a nice murmur. I kept glancing all around and noticed that everyone was dressed up for this event. No one looked like a bum. I relaxed in my chair and took a long pull off my drink. I wanted to enjoy tonight and enjoy the music created by my friend. A random thought wandered in my mind - *what would it have been like if I had dated and married Philippe, rather than move to Moon City and find Clovis?* In all of the time we'd known each other, not once had Philippe ever shown more than brotherly love toward me and I loved him as a sister would. We'd helped each other out many times and when he set off for the world with his music, I felt as though a piece of me was missing. When I later moved to Moon City, I felt that piece return but in another way. I had a new life with Monica and Clovis and honestly, that was all I needed. I sipped on my drink, only to frown when I realized that I drank it all in two gulps. Just then, Angel appeared on the stage, causing much applause and finger snaps, and one person even whistled. He waved his hands to calm the audience down.

"Ladies and gentlemen," he said once it was quiet once more, "I wanna thank you for coming out tonight. We've got a treat for you but then again, that's why you're here, right?" The audience clapped again and Angel grinned widely. "Alright, alright," he said, trying to settle down the crowd, "Fleur de Lis Trio is here with their crazy jazz sounds! You guys ready?"

Someone in the back yelled, "Yes!" causing everyone to laugh.

"Then, without further ado, may I present to you, all the way from *La Nouvelle-Orleans*... LE FLEUR DE LIS TRIO!"

He jumped off the side of the stage just as the trio

appeared onstage, causing everyone to go into a frenzy. I'll admit that even Mooney and I got caught up in it. There was my friend, ready to show us his world. Philippe, Jean, and Leon waved at everyone, and Philippe blew us a kiss, then the trio moved toward their instruments and settled in. I saw Clovis on the side and blew him a kiss. He acted as though he grabbed it and then placed his hand against his chest.

"Thank you, Moon City, for letting us perform for you tonight," Philippe said in his French accent. I knew that several women in the audience would be trying their best to go home with him later, yet I knew my friend. Never liked to fool around unless if it meant more than just one night of fun and frolic. He wanted someone to come home to, someone who was more than just some arm candy. He gave his fellow trio members a good look and a grin, and then they erupted into a fiery number that instantly gave me goose bumps. It's one thing to hear someone play on a record, but it's another creature when you see them perform in person. I felt the electricity jolt from them as they played their instruments and turned it into delicious jazz. You could hear the New Orleans influence, of course, but there was also a dash of general South, some classical music, and even a bit of country. How they did that last part I'll never know, yet it all worked for them. They were alive.

Five songs later, the trio stopped and took their intermission. All three of the members were sweaty yet grinning from ear to ear.

"Alright, *cher*," Philippe yelled into the microphone, "we're gonna take a short break. Go get another drink and smoke and we'll see you soon!" The audience applauded as they left the stage.

"Good lord!" Mooney yelled over the now loud noises

in the club, "They were fantastic!" She lit a cigarette, the first she'd had since the trio started playing, and exhaled long and hard. "Want another drink?"

"Yeah but damn! How many shots were in that last one? I felt really fuzzy!" Monica winked in reply as she got up and made her way to the bar for a refill.

I leaned back in my chair to soak in the flow of the good vibes, only to get up and make my way behind the stage. I wanted to see Philippe for a brief moment and let him know how well they were doing. I looked around, saw Leon and Jean laughing with Clovis, but no Philippe. I then walked through the back door to the alley to the somewhat cool night and noticed Philippe talking with someone.

The street light caused Philippe to glow, while the other person was shrouded in the darkness of the alley. I retraced my steps to give him privacy, only to freeze when I heard Philippe yell out, "No!" I remained frozen, unsure if I needed to close the door as quietly as possible, or listen in when I shouldn't. I remained frozen. Their voices were muffled, yet I saw Philippe moving his hands about wildly while the other figure just stood there. I continued to watch in case he needed help. Philippe calmed down, only to have the other person drop their lit cig to the ground and stub it out with force. I held my breath; the figure then turned around and walked off, leaving Philippe to watch them leave.

Not my business, I thought as I slowly closed the door and returned to my table.

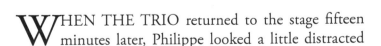

WHEN THE TRIO returned to the stage fifteen minutes later, Philippe looked a little distracted yet wore a gleaming smile for the audience. I peered closer; the smile seemed forced. The trio waved to everyone, and then started with a slower but no less energetic piece. I sipped on my new drink, then eyed Monica who mouthed the words, "Trust me!" It was a small Mai Tai, her favourite drink. I took another sip and noticed that it had less of a punch than my several shots of vodka, but I still took my time in drinking it. As the trio played, I thought about what I witnessed in the alley. I hoped that everything was okay for my friend but judging by the way he played, whatever it was didn't seem to bother him. He tightly closed his eyes and played his sax with so much of himself that it almost seemed forced.

Almost.

—ʍ—

THEY PLAYED FOR a full hour and then called it quits, much to the upset of the audience. I could see that all three members looked beyond worn out yet riding on a natural high. Some of the audience stamped their feet, urging the trio to play just one more song, yet I knew that they were exhausted and starving.

"You flatter us, folks," Philippe seemed to gasp into the microphone, "but we must say *au revoir* to you." Just then, his eyes focused on something toward the back. They widened slightly, then he quickly remembered where he was. He waved his thanks to the audience, as did Jean and Leon, and then the trio disappeared behind the curtains.

"Well," I said to Monica as I finished off my drink, "that was incredible."

"Where's the after party?" Monica asked as she finished off her cigarette. "I'm sure there'll be one."

"I think it's here," I replied as Clovis walked up to us. He didn't look good.

"Ladies, no party tonight," he said with a sigh. "Philippe isn't feeling well and is retiring to his hotel room." He shrugged. "Caught a bug or something." My mind instantly replayed what I witnessed in the alley, then shook it off.

"Can we do anything for him?" I asked. "What about Jean and Leon?"

"They're calling it an early night," Clovis replied. "Seems like this gig wore them out. I'm taking them to their hotel rooms." He kissed my forehead and returned backstage.

"Well, should we have our own party?" Monica asked with a gleam in her eye. "We could always go to Silk." I broke out laughing - Club Silk was the only lesbian bar in town. The only time I was arrested was there. I knew that Clovis wouldn't be home for a while and I really didn't want to be alone right now. I looked at my partner in crime and grinned.

—☙—

CLUB SILK PROVED to be the spot for tonight as well; when we pulled up to the front door, the line to get in was long.

"I'm VIP so no lines," Monica said as we got out after parking her car. I put on my best stroll as we walked up to the club as though we owned it. One look at Monica and the door was quickly opened for us. Almost every table was occupied as the patrons listened to a woman dressed in a floor length green dress sing her heart out while a jazz trio played behind her. I made my way to the bar to order a drink, then turned to see that Monica was standing still and rather close to the stage. After a while, she turned and made her way to my side. I ordered two Mai Tais.

"You okay?" I asked her while we waited. Monica's focus had returned to the stage or rather, the woman performing on it.

"You ever seen such a vision?" she murmured as I handed her her drink.

"Uh-oh," I said with a chuckle, "I think you've got a crush." Mooney turned to face me and winked.

"More than a crush," she replied as she returned her gaze to the woman. "A vision. Gotta ask her out. Hey, Zale!" A burly looking woman dressed like a sailor strolled up to us from behind the bar. I noticed that she was wiping one of the glasses with a rag while a tattoo of an anchor rippled on her arm.

"Hey, Mooney! What's cooking?"

"See that vision of loveliness on the stage? Who is she and is she available?"

Zale cackled and I swear she sounded like a parrot. "That's Joan Sawyer," she replied as she set the clean glass on the counter, only to pick up another one that was wet and began drying it off. "From New York City. First night singing here and I gotta tell ya, she'll be a regular here. Look at all these mooney faced women. Uh, sorry Mooney."

"She's a dream," Mooney replied and I knew that this was more than a crush. "Is she one of us?"

"Hmmm, don't know, but…" Zale looked around to see if anyone was listening, noticed that everyone was focused on Joan, and then pulled us in with her strong arms. "Word is she ran away from some man. Knocked her around for a while. Needed to get away before he axed her." She looked at both of us square in the eye and nodded slowly. "I'll make the introductions after."

She released us from her grip and I took a large sip of my Mai Tai, knowing damn well that I was going to have one hell of a hangover. Monica set her drink to the side and continued to watch Joan perform, enraptured by the siren.

Three songs later, Joan stepped off the stage to much applause and even a dozen red roses and made her way to the bar. Monica gripped my arm as her eyes went wide. She walked right up to an empty spot next to me and waved at Zale. She caressed the roses and then set them carefully on the bar.

"Can I get a club soda with lime?" she asked in a velvet tone that could be heard over the din of the club. I glanced at Monica, who glanced at Zale, and then at me again.

"One club soda with lime," Zale said as she handed the drink to Joan. "Great set, by the way. You probably broke a lot of hearts tonight."

"Thanks, Zale." She cradled her drink with both hands, brought it to her red lips, and drank it all down. She then set the glass on the bar and turned around to face the all-woman crowd. "Looks like a packed house," she said to no one in particular yet I could have sworn there was a hint of sadness in her voice.

"Hey, I wanna introduce you to someone," Zale said just as she placed a hand on Monica's shoulder. "This is Monica Sawyer, photographer and writer of the world." Monica moved from where she stood and approached the woman. She took one of Joan's hands in hers and lightly kissed it.

"*Enchante*," Monica said with nothing but love in her eyes, causing Joan to blush. Monica dropped her hand yet remained by her side.

"And this is, sorry, but I didn't get your name," Zale said to me with a toothy grin plastered on her face.

"Jacqueline Verona, or Jackie," I said as Joan smiled at me.

"I know who you are," Joan said with an even brighter blush. "I've read all your books when I lived in New York." Now it was my turn to blush. "Wow," she added, "I get to meet two famous people in one night. Must be my lucky day." She raised her glass to where a single ice cube perfectly fell into her mouth. She then directly stared at Mooney and cracked the ice without blinking.

Oh boy, I thought. *Maybe I need to get a taxi home.*

"You sing like an angel," Monica said as she moved closer to Joan. "Truly divine."

"Thank you so much," she replied as she placed a hand on Mooney's arm.

Yep, I thought as I finished off my Mai Tai, *I will definitely need a taxi home.*

—⚹—

THANKFULLY, NO COPS arrived to arrest these "wanton women". In fact, I changed my mind and decided to stay at the club, of which Mooney was excited about my change of plans. Even though she was making the moves on Joan, and Joan likewise, she wanted to enjoy her night with her best friend as well. How could I refuse, especially when she started buying more Mai Tais? I knew I had a drinking limit…

As the night wore on and the crowd grew louder and the music got hotter, Joan draped an arm around me and in a very loud whisper said, "I think your friend is awshum!" I nodded in reply because my lips were numb. She giggled and then turned to someone else and proclaimed the same statement. I blinked slowly, at least I think I did, and grinned as Mooney came sashaying up to me with a lit cigarette dangling from her mouth.

"Hey," she said in a surprisingly sober tone, "when're you ready to go home?"

I blinked several times as her words finally sunk into my brain. "Aren't you... you....and Joan?" Hopefully, she understood what I meant.

"She's going home with her roommate and I'm taking you home, my friend," she replied with a grin while that damn cigarette balanced on her bottom lip.

"How in the hell do you do that?" I said with wide eyes while I pointed at her cigarette. "How in the hell?" I then started to laugh because well, why not?

Mooney took a deep drag and then crushed out her cigarette while a stream of smoke jettisoned from her nose as though she was a dragon. She took my arm and gently led me through the crowd of drunk women and out into the night. As soon as a chill breeze wafted through my clothing, I felt the stirrings of sobriety start to creep in. That, or the beginning of a major headache. I groaned and sat on the curb while she obtained her keys, then felt myself being lifted off the ground and soon, we were off.

I sank lower in my seat while Monica drove us back to my home. While the alcohol floated through my body, all I kept thinking was that I wanted to go to bed. I knew that I was going to be sick tomorrow. I closed my eyes, only to feel the car stop and a gloved hand gently touch my shoulder. Before I could slur anything out loud, I felt myself being gently lifted from my seat and back into the night. I heard a man's voice ask how much I drank and then black.

When I opened my eyes again, I felt the sun coming

through the windows. I closed my eyes tightly and then opened them wide. Rolled them around in their sockets and then focused on the window.

Hmmm, I thought as I slowly moved my body up to a seated position in bed. *No headache. No desperate thoughts of wanting to puke.*

I turned my head this way and that with no pain. I grinned and then swung my body to the side of the bed. Nothing. I placed my bare feet on the floor and gently stood up. Still nothing. I looked down to see that someone had undressed me of my night clothes and replaced them with my nightgown.

"Well, well," said Clovis as he entered the room wearing a cat eating a bird grin, "looks like the drunk is up!" He walked toward me with a glass of orange juice and a bottle of aspirin and thrust both toward me. "According to Mooney," he added as I took two pills with the entire glass of juice, "you had quite the night."

"I did and those damn Mai Tais at Club Silk are way too strong!"

Clovis crossed his arms over his chest and sighed. "Okay, she didn't tell me where you guys had gone. Silk again? Any cops?" He smirked and I almost threw my glass at him. He then sat on the bed and pulled me down next to him.

"No, smart guy," I said while still wondering why I wasn't feeling bad, "and in fact, it was a fantastic night to be there. Mooney met someone," I said in a lovey dovey tone. "Singer there named Joan. From New York. Hey baby, why ain't I feeling bad? No headache or anything!"

Clovis looked shocked. "Wait, you don't remember when you puked everything into the toilet?" I stared at him in surprise. "Wow, you were blitzed," he said with a laugh. "After Mooney dropped you off, I carried you to the bathroom where you proceeded to puke everything up. Such a lovely shade of pink."

"Bastard," I said as I lightly punched him in the arm.

"Yeah well, you were trying to punch me while I took off your clothes afterwards. You wanted a fight, go figure."

"I honestly don't remember anything except being led out of the car." I leaned against him and sighed. "Thanks, baby."

"Yeah well, you can thank me later. I'm heading to Philippe's hotel room." Suddenly, I sat up straight.

"How's he feeling? What happened?"

"Don't know but I think it's exhaustion. I know what it's like. You go and go and go until you're literally crawling on the floor, weak like a kitten. He and the guys had been going strong for months without taking a break. No wonder he looked so winded and stressed."

Clovis kissed my forehead and helped me to the bed again, then left with promises of cooking tonight. I blew him a kiss and then relaxed in bed as my head sunk deep into the pillows. I closed my eyes…

Philippe playing his heart out…
Philippe yelling at someone in the alley.…
Philippe looking stressed…
No!

My eyes flew open as that one word vibrated in my mind. I slowly got out of bed and then walked into the bathroom to take a long bubble bath. I stripped off my nightgown and sat on the side of the tub while watching the tub fill up with bubbles and hot water. I then stepped in and turned off the water, allowing the water to melt away the cobwebs in my brain.

Who was that person he was talking to? And why did he

look so stressed when he returned? I sunk deeper and allowed myself to melt.

After resting in the tub, followed by a good scrub, I got dressed and left the house. When I jumped into the car, I had only one thought - to ask Philippe who that person was last night. I slipped on my cat eye sunglasses and headed toward the hotel. As I drove, I turned on the radio to the local jazz station. For some reason, I needed to calm down my nerves but I wasn't sure why. Why did I feel so strange? I had puked up all of the alcohol, leaving me slightly dehydrated but that was it. Yet, I couldn't stop thinking that something was wrong with my friend. By the time I reached the hotel, I saw Clovis standing outside and knew. Clovis saw me pull up and immediately raced to my door and opened it before I could even turn it off.

"He's gone," he said in a loud tone, then started to pace.

I shut the door and leaned against my car. *Gone?* "Where's Leon and Jean?" I asked, causing him to stop in his tracks.

"They're in their rooms and they don't know where he is!" Clovis resumed pacing as he stuck a cig in his mouth and tried to light it. I walked toward my husband and grabbed his shoulders to get him to face me.

"Wait, aren't we blowing this up for no reason?" I said in a gentle tone while trying hard to feel that calm. "Maybe he left for breakfast and'll be back soon."

"Delight, he paid for his room and just left!" He lit his cig while I frowned. No, this didn't seem like my friend at all. I returned to my car and leaned against it while I crossed my arms. "Did he mention anything about leaving early?" I asked my pacing husband.

"Nothing! He felt worn out and wanted to return to his room. He said that he wanted to have lunch with you and me today. Damn it!" Clovis had burned his lip and angrily threw the cig to the ground. "Did he tell you anything, Jackie?"

I shook my head while that image of him talking with someone in the alley returned. "Um, Clovis?" He stopped pacing and stared at me. "I saw him last night in the alley," I said in a shaking voice. "He seemed to be fighting with someone. Any idea?"

He didn't say anything to me," Clovis replied as he lit up another cig. "Said he needed to get some air. That's all." He rushed toward me and said in a tense voice, "Do you think . . ." I didn't want him to finish that thought, only because I was thinking it too. I pulled Clovis into my arms and held him.

"We'll find him," I said as I stroked his head. "He's probably out doing whatever. Maybe he just paid early." I pulled away from Clovis and tried to smile. "Maybe he met some chick last night and didn't want to tell you or the guys." I could see Clovis trying to accept my words. "He's always been somewhat private when it came to matters of the heart," I added, yet I didn't feel right in saying them. "Trust me," I finished as I got in my car, "he'll be back soon. Call me when he does, okay?"

Clovis didn't look convinced and I knew where it came from - the death of his only sister, Dianne. Ever since he found out that his sister had been murdered, he panicked whenever someone he cared about disappeared. He leaned down and kissed me, then pulled away and walked toward the hotel while smoking like a chimney. I watched him and then drove off. I had to see Mooney.

—◆—

AS I DROVE through the streets of Moon City, my thoughts were all over the place. Philippe disappearing, Philippe smiling at me, me getting drunk at Club Silk, Joan singing her heart out. It was a beautiful day, yet it was nothing as I got deeper in my thoughts. I arrived at Mooney's house before I knew it. I pulled as close as possible to the curb and then turned off the car. I sat in the car and gripped the steering wheel as tightly as possible, then released it with a loud exhale.

"Get it together," I told myself as I looked into my eyes in the rear view window. I got out and made my way up to Monica's house. It used to bother me to visit her because she lived in the richer area of Moon City, yet I realized that she was the real deal of being a friend and not some fake, I knew I had a true friend. She liked the finer things in life but she wasn't a snob about it. I rang her doorbell and took a step back to wait. Seconds later, the door flew open to reveal Mooney dressed in a black robe and her black frame glasses.

"Well, well," she said as she ushered me inside, "good to know you're not dead! Want a drink?"

"Are you kidding me?" I said while laughing as I made my way to her living room and sat down on her couch.

Monica joined me and reached for a glass of water from a side table. "How do ya feel?"

"Like a million dollars," I replied and meant it.

"Well, not everyone has your constitution," she replied with a small groan. She finished off her water and said, "I really thought I could handle last night but I guess my age is catching up with me."

"Mooney, you're only 25," I said.

She rolled her eyes and then placed a hand over her eyes. "Come over here to gloat?"

"Hardly," I replied in a sober tone. "Seen Philippe since last night?"

Mooney removed her hand from her now clear and serious eyes. "What d'ya mean?"

"I mean, he's missing. Just came from the hotel and Clovis was freaking out."

"When you say missing, what do you mean?" She sat up straight and crossed her legs as her eyes focused on me and my attempt to explain what I didn't know.

"I mean that he paid for his room early, packed up his clothes, and left," I replied. "No clue where he went, but I'm thinking he just got breakfast or is with some chick."

"Perhaps," Monica replied as she tapped her fingernail against her chin, "or…"

"Oh no," I said while waving my hands no, "let's not even say anything bad." I looked around at her moderately decorated living room and sighed. "He'll show up." Monica stared at me with a look that said, *No, he won't.* "By the way," I added, "I saw him arguing with someone in the alley last night during their break."

"Hmmm, any idea who it was?"

"None. Couldn't see or hear them. All I heard was Philippe yelling out the word No. I left before they saw me."

"I wonder who that person was," Monica murmured. "Does he know anyone here, aside from you and Clovis?" I shook my head no. "Then, let's assume that he met some chick or something."

"But if that was true, he would have told me," I replied, canceling out what I had just said seconds ago. "We're tight."

"Yeah yeah, but maybe he didn't meet some woman. Ummm, Jackie, did he have any enemies?" Those words fell into my stomach like a rock. Enemies? I shook my head no but I couldn't be sure.

"As far as I know, he was a clean jazz player," I said slowly. "Treated people well, close family ties, and no lingering women who wanted revenge on him for leaving them. He loved jazz, loved New Orleans, and loved his family. He read more than me too!" Monica smiled. "Seriously though, he had no problems. Damn golden boy."

"Yeah well, you haven't seen or heard from him in several years," Monica offered and I had to agree. "Who knows what could have happened in that period of time." She got up with her usual fluid grace. "Want coffee? Even if you say no, I'm still making a pot." I sighed as she strolled into the kitchen, leaving me with my thoughts and our lingering conversation that wasn't over at all. Knowing Monica, if there was something that interested her, she wouldn't let go of it until it was handled or it went away.

She returned with a tray bearing two cups of coffee, a sugar jar, and a small pitcher of cream. She set the tray on the table before us and proceeded to prepare my coffee.

"So," I asked in trying to change the subject, "anything between you and Joan? I was ready to get a taxi and leave you two alone." Monica said nothing but handed me my cup of coffee, then proceeded to prepare hers. "Um, earth to Monica," I said in a joking manner, "talk to me." She leaned back in the couch and took a sip of her coffee.

"Joan's a sweet girl," Monica replied, "yet this is more important." Her eyes showed that she was serious. "Remember when we came together that last time?" I nodded yes. "Seems like we've got another mystery to possibly solve." I took a deep sip of my coffee and enjoyed the roll of flavors in my mouth. *And*, I thought with a sigh, *she was right. No one just ups and leaves without telling their friends goodbye.* "I'm sure there's a reasonable answer," Monica added, "but for now, he's missing after paying his hotel bill. I mean, what kind of crazy musician would just leave without telling his band mates, or his friends? I'm tellin' ya, there's more." She took another sip of her coffee. "There always is." As much as I didn't want Mooney to be right, she was right.

"I'm starving," I replied as I finished off my coffee. "Wanna grab some breakfast downtown?"

"I'll cook," Mooney replied and then got up and whisked away to the kitchen before I could say no. I quickly jumped up with coffee in hand and joined her in the kitchen, where I found her placing bread in the toaster. "And yes, I did hit it off with Joan," she replied, causing me to grin. She turned and gave me a wink, then moved to the refrigerator to grab some eggs. "I do like her, Jackie. I really want to see where this goes, if anything. She's supposed to be coming over for dinner tomorrow."

"You sly minx," I said, causing Mooney to throw a towel at me. "Seriously, I'm happy for you. Can't wait to hear how that dinner'll turn out."

"Me too! But, in getting back to your friend," Mooney replied as she cracked the eggs against her pan, "has he ever done anything like this before that you can remember?"

"Not really," I replied thoughtfully. "I just want to hear that he's okay. That's all." I sipped my coffee and frowned at the now cold liquid. I returned to the living room and plopped down on the couch.

Oh, Philippe, I thought as I tried hard not to cry.

—⁂—

THE PHONE CALL came right as we were in the middle of breakfast. Mooney looked at me and I looked at her, then we both jumped up and raced toward the phone. She picked it up.

"Mooney? Is Jackie there?" I heard Clovis ask and she handed the phone to me. "Delight? Oh thank god, he's fine!" I grinned from ear to ear, letting Mooney know that it was good news. "That bastard…damn, Jackie, he bought a house!"

I gripped the phone tighter. "House? What? Where? Um…why?"

"Easy, baby, easy. He bought a house here in Moon City."

"What?" Monica tugged on my sleeve and I nodded to let her know that I would tell her everything. "Here?"

"Yeah, he likes it here so much that he decided to make it his home. That's where he was today. Had the cash and just did it."

"Okay, well I'll be home after breakfast. We can talk more later. Are you still with him?"

"I'm still at the hotel. He went upstairs to tell Jean and Leon. Wait, here he comes. Love you, Delight!" We hung up and I felt my entire body go limp. I sat on the couch and Mooney joined me.

"House here?" she asked.

"Let's finish breakfast and I'll tell you what Clovis told me." We returned to our breakfast turned celebratory meal as I filled Mooney in with what Clovis had told me. When I finished, my friend bit off a huge piece of her toast and chewed thoughtfully.

"Wow, so he bought a house and no one knew about it. Crazy." Although I was glad that my friend was okay, I was also in a little bit of shock. He loved New Orleans and told me on many occasions that he would never live anywhere else, except Paris. Suddenly, my friend would be living here in Moon City! "I wonder if Fleur de Lis will still be around," Mooney wondered aloud just as I was thinking the same thing. That jazz trio was his lifeblood, his reason for getting out of bed. As much as he loved his family, he loved his trio even more.

"Let's go see him today," I suggested, to which Monica nodded yes. Although I was glad to know that my friend was safe, I still had questions. For instance, that scene in the alley way.

———※———

WHILE MOONEY GOT dressed, I called our house and Clovis picked up on the second ring.

"Hey baby, is Philippe still with you?"

"Hey Delight and yes he is! I'm looking at him."

"Great! Mooney and I will be home soon. She's getting dressed."

"Oh boy, that'll take forever!"

"Hush and I love you." I hung up the phone just as an unsettled feeling crept into my stomach. I placed a hand over my stomach in trying to calm it down. Was I still drunk and didn't know it? All of the delicious breakfast would have settled and soaked up the remaining alcohol. I pressed a little firmer and soon enough, it quieted down. Mooney soon appeared in the living room, wearing blue jeans and a red sweater. "You look like a high schooler," I said as she stuck her tongue out at me and grabbed her car keys. We were soon off.

Thankfully, Mooney decided to take her own car, giving

me a chance to be alone while I drove home. That strange fluttering did not return, yet my mind was buzzing with a million questions for my French friend. I soon arrived home and parked my car on the sidewalk, just as Mooney arrived and pulled up behind me. We both got out of our cars and I noticed that we both had the same look - unreadable. We walked toward the front door, only to stop when we heard some laughing loudly. I unlocked the door and let us in, only to see Clovis sitting on the floor with a cup of tea next to him and a cig dangling from his mouth. Philippe sat on the couch, holding a glass of milk, and was still in the process of laughing. He quieted down when he saw us walk in.

"Jackie!" he said as he set his milk on the coffee table and jumped up to hug me. I returned the enthusiasm as I hugged him back. "Look, I wanna say that I'm sorry for scaring you like that," He added when we pulled away. "I really didn't mean to. Honest." He glanced over my shoulder to see Monica and gave her a warm smile. He then led me to the couch and we both sat down. Monica joined Clovis on the floor and immediately pulled out her cigarette case.

"Alright, Mister," I said in a mock stern tone, "tell me everything!" He drank from his milk, wiped his mouth with the back of his hand and began.

"I wanna say again that I'm sorry-"

"Great," I replied, "but spill."

He blushed and nodded his head yes. "Fine, fine, jeez! Anyway, when we arrived in Moon City, I actually took a little taxi tour of the city to locate a bookstore. When I finally located one, I walked in and enjoyed some good quality time there. Picked up some books for the road. I knew that Jean and Leon weren't readers, so it was all me. When my taxi returned me to my hotel, I couldn't help but take in the city and all it had to offer. A thought sprouted in my head, one that stayed with me all through the gig the other night." He took my hands in his and gave me such a look that I wanted to look away. "Jackie, I fell in love with Moon City. And she, with me."

"But," I started, "New Orleans and Paris are your loves, not here!"

"I know, I know, but experience can change a man. I want something different for me. This city is something different." He glanced away for a moment, but not before I saw something gleam in his eyes. "New Orleans is filled with *histoire* and ghosts. That city stays in the past because to move forward is to let go of that which holds them back. They punish that which they don't understand." I was shocked - who was this man sitting across from me? "I called my family and told them of my choice. They understood, thank god."

"What about Fleur de Lis?" Monica asked as a cloud of smoke blanketed her face.

"Oh, I've got plans for that," he replied in a vague tone. "Anyway, I...uh...need to confess. I wasn't ill the night of the gig." I glared at him and snatched my hands from his. "I needed time to think, so I waited until everyone left or went to their hotel room, then took a long walk through the city. I needed to clear my head and staying in my room wasn't it. I wanted to see Moon City and walking around was the answer."

"I get it," Clovis said, now joining in, "but damn, man!"

"I wanted to be alone and just walk, ya know? I walked until I felt like my feet were gone. That's when I found this house on Ulysses Street." I glanced at Mooney just as she glanced at me - that was the street where Sylvain and his beatnik tribe lived. Sylvain had dated Clovis' sister and then broke it off with her so that he could date some art student chick. Some time later, she was killed. That street did not have good memories for me. I glanced at Clovis and noticed that his face was like a mask. I knew what he was thinking of as well. "Cute little bungalow and for sale. I raced back to the hotel and set my alarm for 6 am. When I woke up the next day, I took a taxi to the house again, checked it out, and then decided to purchase it." He took my hands again and I let him. "I called up the agent and told him that I wanted it right then and there. At first, he thought I was crazy, but then when I told him who I was and that I was going to pay all of it in cash, well, you can imagine what he thought. It was made in the shade." He finished his milk and let out a little burp.

"That's great and all," I said, ready to start with my questions, "but what are you going to do with Fleur de Lis? What did Jean and Leon say to you moving here?"

"Ah, yeah," he said with a sad smile. "Sorry to say but Fleur de Lis is no more, at least, with me at the helm." We were all quiet for literally a minute and then hell broke loose.

"What the hell?"

"Are you crazy?!"

"Man, what?"

Philippe looked at each of us as we sputtered our thoughts, only to raise a hand to silence us. "Join the crowd," he said. "Jean and Leon didn't take it too well either, but I told them to not tell anyone until it was made official."

"So, you're just giving up the trio just like that?" Monica asked, snapping her fingers for emphasis. He nodded yes. "What are they gonna do now?"

He shrugged. "They're kinda upset with me right now. I'm lettin' them cool down their heads. As far as I know, they're returning to New Orleans. Let 'em."

I was shocked. *The end of Fleur de Lis Trio?*

"Man, why didn't you tell me this earlier?" Clovis asked as I could see his anger rising. "I mean, man!"

"That was part of that walk," Philippe replied as we calmed down to hear the rest. "I've been on tour for years and yeah, it's outta sight, but after a while, it gets to ya." He hung his head low. "I got worn out, man. Beat. I wanted a break. I'm getting one."

"Most musicians are like that," Monica stated, "so they take a vacation or time off to do just that. They don't just quit when it's going well for them!" She stubbed out her cigarette in the ashtray with a little more force than needed.

"But what if you realized that maybe, you wanted something else in your life?" Philippe countered. I fell quiet. "I've been searchin' for something else for most of my life and didn't know it. Well, after coming here and walking the streets, I know now. I want a different life. And it starts today." He blinked several times and then stared right at me. I noticed that his left eye twitched. I'd never seen him so serious before; his intense stare almost scared me, except that it was my friend and not some stranger.

"Well," Mooney stated as she finished her cigarette, " if that's what you want to do with your life, then welcome to Moon City." She smiled a weak smile and then our eyes locked again. She could tell I was upset, yet honestly I couldn't really be angry with him. I know I was feeling selfish in wanting Fleur de Lis Trio to remain a trio. It was his life, after all. He made the choice to become a jazz musician. He could also make the choice to leave the business. I glanced at Clovis and knew that he was angry and confused - to leave at the height of your music career seemed crazy, not to mention foolish. Although my husband was quite successful with the Professor Trio, he was nowhere near the level that Fleur de Lis had obtained.

"Man, do whatever," Clovis said as he got up and walked toward the kitchen, "but as for me, I don't get it and never will." He walked in, only to pop his head out again to add, "Don't expect me to support you, either." He darted back to the kitchen as Mooney and I both sighed.

"I didn't expect for him to understand," Philippe said as he shook his head sadly, "but thanks, Monica, for your words. Jackie?"

"No matter what you decide," I said with little difficulty, "I will always be your friend. I may not agree," I added, causing him to grin, "but at least you'll be living in the same city as me." Deep down inside of me was another matter - *unease*. "Hey," I said, trying to be light about it, "I didn't want to tell you this, but I saw you in an argument with someone the night of the concert." For a brief moment, Philippe's smooth face cracked and then quickly repaired itself.

"Oh?"

"Yeah," I said as I warmed up to confessing my spying on him, "I didn't hear anything, only you yelling the word 'no'." I laid a hand on his and noticed that it was trembling. "You seemed out of sorts when you did the second set. Everything okay?"

"Yeah, yeah," he replied a little too hastily. "Someone who claimed they knew my family was trying to get some cash from me."

"Did you actually know him?" Monica asked.

He glanced in her direction and then his eyes returned to me and only me. They unsettled me . . . "Yeah," he grumbled, "I knew him. Poor slob. He was travelling through and heard that I was playing here, so he waited for me to take a cig break. Couldn't afford a ticket or something. He pleaded with me, knowing that I'm well off, and claimed that he kept in touch with my family. That's what did it for me. Don't drag my family in like a lifeboat when you're drowning."

"What happened to him?" I asked.

"Ah, I ended up giving him five dollars and he split or so I thought. When we returned for the second set, I saw him in the back of the club, grinning at me. I guess he just wanted to get into the club or something. Anyway, he left after that. I felt like a damn fool."

"It happens," I said with relief as I pulled my hand away. "Now, since you live here now, we need to celebrate our new resident!" Philippe grinned widely as a single tear formed in his eye and slid down his face. He quickly brushed it away. "That happy about living here?" I asked with mock sarcasm.

"Nah, it's just that, well, it feels good to belong somewhere, ya know? I got New Orleans and all but this place, Moon City, this is all on me. No family members with their names and titles, no one greasing someone's palm with old money." Another tear fell down his face. "I worked hard to be where I am now. I want more of that." He took both my hands in his and squeezed tightly, almost painfully. "I'm home," he whispered.

I THOUGHT THAT it would be weird to return to Ulysses Street, yet once we turned the corner and slowly drove, I felt nothing. Dianne was long gone, as was her killer. As we approached Sylvain's house, I wondered if he and his crazy bunch of artists still lived there.

"Mine is the last house on the right," Philippe instructed Mooney as I continued to look out from the rear window. Yeah, there was his house and . . I gasped. Sylvain was sitting on the steps, smoking a cig and staring at our car drive by. I wondered for a moment if he recognized it, yet he soon put out his cig and went inside without any kind of recognition. I wondered about Ansel and his goat, yet it faded once we pulled up to Philippe's house and got out.

The house was a simple one story bungalow painted brown and blue, complete with a porch and a small yard in front. Philippe grinned from ear to ear as he raced up the stairs and unlocked the door for us. Mooney slipped her arm through mine as we walked up the stairs, while Philippe dashed inside.

"He's really excited about his new house," I said.

"Yeah," was her reply.

I lowered my voice. "What's up?" I asked her.

"Ready to be Sherlock and Watson again?" We reached the front door before I could answer her, yet I knew what the answer would be. As much as I was happy to have my friend move to Moon City, it still didn't sit right with me and apparently Mooney too. Yet, I dropped the matter as we walked into the empty house. Philippe joined us from the back and gave us the tour: two bedrooms, one nice sized kitchen, living room, a small room that would make a perfect library, and a larger yard out back. White walls that were ready for their new owner to express himself.

"I have to admit," Mooney said as we returned to the front room, "I'm impressed."

"Yeah, got it for a steal," he replied as he wandered into the kitchen, leaving us two to meander through. My eyes took in everything, including a side door in the hallway by the bedrooms.

"Hey," I yelled to Philippe, "where's this side door go to?" Instantly, he raced from the kitchen to us and leaned against the door in some attempt to look cool.

"Basement," he replied as his eyes looked down at his shoes. "It's a mess down there. I wanted to brick it up and make it an entertainment room or a cellar to store wine. Dunno."

"Oooh, creepy," Monica said as she reached for the door knob, to which Philippe slapped her hands away. "Hey!" she yelled as she rubbed her hands, "what gives? Just wanted to check out the creep factor down there."

"Whoever lived here before really didn't care about the basement," Philippe replied as he stood firm against the door. "But…be my guest." Surprisingly, he moved away and gave us access. Mooney glared at him for a moment, then turned the knob and opened the door. Cold, musty air greeted us. Monica reached out and felt for a light switch.

"Light doesn't work," he said, only to gasp when the lights clicked on. Monica grinned with satisfaction as she descended the stairs with me following her. As we walked down, I took a good look around and saw the usual basement details - cobwebs everywhere, creaky wooden staircase, and piles of dusty boxes from floor to ceiling all over the place. We reached the bottom and I immediately wanted to return upstairs.

"Satisfied?" I asked as Monica took a good look around the basement.

"Still waiting on a skeleton to jump out at us, but yeah!" I rolled my eyes and then returned upstairs with her behind me. When we reached the top stair, we found Philippe leaning against the opposite wall with crossed arms.

"Satisfied?" he also asked Mooney. She stared at him in silence and then slowly nodded, then walked out of the house. "What's with her?" he asked me. I shrugged and then followed her outside. I found her leaning against her car with a lit cig in hand. Her eyes narrowed when I approached.

"Alright," I asked as I lit one as well and stood next to her, "talk."

"I dunno," she said as she blew out a perfect smoke ring. "I'm just feeling something." She looked at me and added, "And you are too, aren't you?" I took a deep inhale and exhaled through my nose.

"You're right," I replied calmly as I watched Philippe lock up the house and approach us, "It's time for Sherlock and Watson again."

—◦◦◦—

"THANKS FOR MEETING me," I told Jean and Leon as we slid into the booth at Lucy's Diner. The small restaurant was perfect for our meeting. Several days after viewing Philippe's house, I told Mooney that I wanted to talk with the other members of the now defunct Fleur de Lis Trio. Maybe they knew why their leader suddenly went AWOL on them; then again, maybe they wouldn't. I was surprised that they were still in town; according to Jean, they wanted to stay for several days in case their former leader changed his mind and wanted to return to jazz.

"Hey, no problem, *cher*," Jean said with, I swear to god, a twinkle in his eyes. "Maybe we aren't the best people to talk with, ya know?"

"Look, all I know is that your leader is acting really funny and I just want to make sure that there's nothing else going on," I said just as the waitress, an older black woman, approached our table with menus. She gave all three of us a good look as she handed the menus to us, then left us alone.

"What's her problem?" Leon asked as he stared at her retreating form. "Huh. You'd think she'd never seen three adults sitting at a booth."

I shrugged; now was not the time to get off track. "Who knows? Anyway, how was he during the tour?"

"His usual self," Jean replied, then slowly nodded as he tapped his ear with one of his long fingers. "Wait…Leon, remember that one night in Chicago?"

"Oh yeah," Leon replied as his eyes lit up with the memory. "As we got ready for that night, I saw Philippe talking with someone at a small table in the back of the club. Didn't think anything about it, until I looked again. Swear to *mon dieu*, I was seeing double! I saw him . . . and someone who looked just like him." He shook his head again. "My eyesight isn't that great, so I got Jean to check it out."

"All those women you've been ogling caused you to go blind," Jean said with a chuckle. "I keep telling you to get glasses! Hey, we'd better look at our menus before she returns." We put our talk to a halt, yet my mind was racing - double? Someone who looked like Philippe? I checked out the menu and saw a lovely tuna melt casserole that was just calling to me. The waitress returned five minutes later with glasses of water for us. As she handed the glasses to us, she eyed each of us intently. We handed our menus to her in silence. Leon couldn't take it any longer.

"Say, *cher*," he said as his New Orleans accent came out in full force, "what's with the looks? Did we, how you say, offend you?"

"Where you from?" she asked with a hint of suspicion.

"Well, I and the other man are from *La Nouvelle-Orleans*," Leon replied in a sweet as sugar voice, "and that lovely madame is from here."

She turned to look at me, almost stared, and then said, "I ain't never seen such fine looking people like you." She then grinned. "It's just . . . nice." She pulled out her order book and pencil. "And you, with that accent, ain't you something?"

"Are you from here too?" I asked with relief.

"Nah, I came from Alabama five years ago. Wanted to get away, ya know? You guys are the second group I've seen so refined and all lately. The last one, well, he was a mess but he tipped me well. Claimed he was a musician." I perked up. "He had that accent like you, sir. Both he and his friend."

"Friend?" I asked while trying to keep myself calm. "We need to order, too."

The waitress grinned and waved her hand to shush me. "Don't need to do that," she replied. "I know what each of you should try here. Anyway," she said as she leaned against the booth, "his friend looked really bad, ya know? Like he hadn't slept in a week or sumthin'."

"What did he look like, the friend?" I asked. My knees started to shake.

"Be right back," she replied as she left us to handle another table. I smacked my fist in my hand.

"Jean, did you get a good look at the other man that night?" I asked.

"Yeah, and she's right - he looked terrible. Hat pulled somewhat down, covering part of his face."

"That's 'cause he put it on after I ran off to get you," Leon replied a little angry. "Jackie, I swear, he looked just like Philippe."

"Then I wonder if that was the same person I saw in the

alley way the night of the gig here," I mused.

"Did you see his face?" Leon asked. I shook my head. "Well, at least we know that there was somebody talking to Philippe."

"Yeah, but would that cause him to freak out and then later quit the trio?' I asked. "Does he have any debts or anything?"

"Nah," Jean replied. "No debts, nothing. Clean and straight." I fell quiet and drank my water. "By the way," he added, "we had no idea that he would leave the trio. From how he talked, he loved all of it - traveling, playing in different cities, making people happy with the jazz."

"Did he ever talk about going home?"

"That's the funny thing," Leon jumped in. "He told us he never wanted to return there. Said he wanted a clean break of that city." I leaned back in my seat. *Maybe I'm getting upset for nothing,* I thought. *Maybe he just wants a change.* Our waitress returned after some time with three full plates on a tray. She handed them to us with silverware. Mine was meatloaf with mashed potatoes and asparagus, Jean's was a thick slice of lasagna with a hefty piece of garlic bread, and Leon's was fried chicken with two biscuits.

"Anyway," our waitress resumed as we dove into our food, "that musician left me a big tip! His friend . . . all he had was some coffee. Black. Had me refill it three times."

"Thanks for telling us this," I said as I ate another chunk of the mouthwatering meatloaf.

"Shucks, ain't nothin'," she replied as she looked around at the almost empty place. "I'm Vera, by the way. Nice to meet y'all."

"I'm Jackie and that man you're talking about is my friend." I wonder just how much to tell her. "We've," I glanced at Jean and Leon, "been worried about him. Good to know he seemed alright."

"Oh yeah, he did, but his friend . . ." She trailed off for a minute and then said, "I do remember that his friend, the one that looked so bad, looked at me and smiled. I've never seen a smile like that as long as I live. He looked spooked." She looked around again to see if anyone was looking for her, then leaned in. We all stopped eating. "Like the Devil got him or something." We glanced at each other and I could tell that the thought of eating left all of us. "'Course, I'm just talkin', ya know. But those eyes," Vera said with a little shiver. "I hope I never see that guy again. His friend can come in any time he wants!"

"Well, he's bought a house here, so I'll let him know," I said with a wink, letting her know that she was cool with us. She wandered off to help with a family that just walked into the restaurant. When she was clear out of earshot, I asked, "Well, what do you guys think?"

"I think that whoever this guy is, he's probably gone," Leon replied and Jean nodded.

"Philippe told me that it was a friend of his from New Orleans, one who needed money and was down on his luck." Both men relaxed as they picked up their forks again.

"Yeah, I've seen both men and women try to swindle some cash from him, and every time he told them no," Jean said. "Seems like this guy was the same." He shook his head and then finished off his lasagna. I knew that everything was cool now. Everything I was told seemed to fall into place. Philippe, for lack of a better term, decided to split from his previous life and create a new one. That's all. I finished my glass of water.

"So, what will you guys do now?" I asked after a while.

Leon shrugged while Jean replied, "Probably return home and start up a new trio. It doesn't look like Philippe's joining us." He looked at Leon. "Wanna try a second time? Two French Guys." Leon finished off his meal and then wiped his mouth with his napkin.

"Sure, as long as I can give it a better name than that!" I knew that they would want to be leaving soon, and yet I didn't want to see them go. They felt like extended family to me. And still, they had no reason to remain in Moon City if Philippe had decided to make his home here. Vera returned one more time to collect our empty plates.

"Y'all want any dessert?" she asked. Jean and Leon pleaded that they couldn't eat another bite, yet my sweet tooth called to me. I asked her what they had. "Hmmm, we got pecan pie, bread pudding -"

"I'll take the bread pudding," I replied with a grin. She whisked off to take care of my request. "Sorry, but I'm using my sweet tooth as an excuse to keep you guys here longer," I admitted with a sheepish grin.

"Hey, no worries, *cher*," Jean replied as he leaned back in his seat. "We've got nowhere else to go, right Leon?"

"True," Leon said thoughtfully, "but we've got to talk with our booking guy about this. I don't know how he'll take it. *Merde*," he muttered quietly. I had to agree with him - Philippe's act really messed everything up.

"How long have you guys known him?" I asked.

"Oh, I've known him for only five years," Leon replied.

"About five years for me too," Jean added. Something was forming in the back of my mind. Vera brought my bread pudding five minutes later. I ate it, all the while a plan formed in my mind. As much as I liked Jean and Leon, I didn't want to tell them what was going through my mind. I had a hunch. A wild hunch.

—◦◦◦—

AFTER WE LEFT the diner and went our separate ways, I drove to Philippe's new house. Although I tried to keep myself cool, I was a bundle of nerves. I arrived fifteen minutes later and pulled up next to the sidewalk. My hands were sweaty, so I wiped them on my skirt, then got out and slowly made my way up the stairs. When I reached the door, I gently knocked and then stood back. No one came to the door. I waited for another minute, then peered through the windows. No one and no furniture in the rooms. I waited for another minute and then tried the door knob. The door opened with a soft click. I glanced around, making sure no one saw me, and then walked in.

"Hello? Philippe?" I called out as I crept through the empty living room, "It's Jackie! Your door was unlocked." No answer. I turned toward the front door, only to stop as I heard a muffled sound. I resumed my slow walk through the house as I followed the noise. As I walked through each room, I noticed that there was no sign of anyone living here. No papers, no furniture, not even a dirty cup of coffee sitting on a counter. I stopped to listen for the sound. Several seconds passed by in silence and then I heard it again. Was that the sound of . . . I crept along until I reached the door leading to the basement. I slowly opened the door, and the sound grew. *Yeah*, I thought to myself as I froze by the open door. *It's the sound of someone shoveling.* I closed the door, trying hard not to make any more noise, then turned around and left. I didn't realize I'd been holding my breath until I reached my car. I exhaled loudly and then sighed as I got in and drove off. I was lucky that no one saw me.

I reached home and quickly ran inside and fell on my couch.

"Hey, Delight," Clovis said as he entered the room, only to stop and give me a good look over. "You look spooked," he said with concern.

"Um, baby," I started, feeling foolish for what I was about to tell him, "I went to Philippe's house."

Clovis put his hands on his hips and sighed. "What did you do now?"

"Nothing, nothing but…uh… I went in and he didn't know."

"You what?"

"Easy, baby, easy," I replied in a cool tone. "I know it was stupid, but well, sit down." Clovis eyed me for a minute and then carefully sat down next to me.

"Spill," he said as he lit a cig. I joined him.

"I met up with Jean and Leon," I started, "and we got to talking about Philippe. Did you know that he never wanted to return to New Orleans?" Clovis almost dropped his cig on his jeans. "Guess you didn't," I said. I filled him in on what they had told me earlier, followed by what Vera had just randomly told us. When I finished, I realized that my cig had burned all the way down to the filter.

"Well," Clovis said slowly, "it does explain why he's acting so kooky. Shame that the trio is breaking up, but glad that Jean and Leon are keeping true to the music. No idea about the other guy, huh?"

"Nothing," I replied in frustration. "You haven't seen any weird cat walking around, have you?"

"Nope, just the usual citizens of our fine city." He grinned. "Now," he said, suddenly turning serious, "explain why you were at his house?"

I cleared my throat. "Well, for one, there's no furniture there."

"That's normal, Delight," Clovis countered. "He just bought the house, ya know."

"Yeah, but there's *nothing* in the house! No paper, no signs of living there, not even dirty dishes. When I walked in, I took a good look around. I did hear a strange sound coming from the basement. Sounded like someone was shoveling."

"Shoveling."

I shook my head. "I know it sounds weird, baby, but trust me. I heard what I heard."

"All right, all right," Clovis replied with a grin, "I know you, Miss Jacqueline. When you get an idea, you don't let go of it."

"It was stupid of me to go in there, yet . . ." Yet what, I wondered. Why did I still feel like there was something else? "It's my nerves," I added.

"Sounds like you need a cup of Darjeeling," Clovis replied as he got up and sauntered into the kitchen, while I tried to relax. Just then, our phone rang, causing me to jump. I laughed it off and then picked up.

"Jackie? Jackie?" It was Mooney and she didn't sound right. Maybe her dinner with Joan turned out better than expected.

"Hey, what's goin' on?"

"Can you come by my house in an hour?"

"Sure but why?"

"Just come by in an hour." She hung up before I said okay.

I jumped up and raced into the kitchen to find Clovis steadily making our tea. He turned, saw my face, and then said, "Now what?" I told him about Mooney's strange and short phone call, to which he replied, "you've got an hour." He handed me a cup of Darjeeling. "Drink this." I leaned against the counter with cup in hand and sighed. "Did she tell you anything?" he asked as he leaned next to me. I shook my head no. "Then, don't worry about it, Delight. You've been on edge ever since you found out about Philippe's plans." He stared into his steaming cup. "To tell you the truth, I wish he hadn't told you anything."

"Me too." We drank our tea in silence.

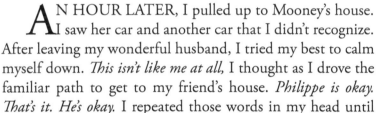

AN HOUR LATER, I pulled up to Mooney's house. I saw her car and another car that I didn't recognize. After leaving my wonderful husband, I tried my best to calm myself down. *This isn't like me at all,* I thought as I drove the familiar path to get to my friend's house. *Philippe is okay. That's it. He's okay.* I repeated those words in my head until I reached Mooney's house. I parked and then made my way to her front door. I knocked once and the door flew open, revealing Detective Hancock!

"Wow, are you finally arresting Mooney?" I joked, only to fall quiet when I saw his face.

"I wish I didn't need to say this," he said as he moved to the side to let me in, "but I need your and her help." We walked into the living room to find Monica looking tense as she sat on the edge of her couch. I sat down next to her as my stomach turned. "Last night, I received a report about an escaped patient from an asylum in Louisiana," Hancock said as he remained standing, his grim face staring at the both of us. "Not only was there an escape, but one of the staff members was murdered. A young nurse."

"Well, that's terrible to hear but why you?" I asked while afraid of the answer. "Louisiana is so far away from here."

Hancock ran a hand down his face and sighed. "We get reports like this all the time, honestly. But, in the case of you two," he said, then paused, "do you know a Philippe Vervain?" I wanted to faint, but instead lit a cig. Mooney could see that my hands were trembling. "It's a family member that's escaped."

"Jackie," Mooney said softly, "do you think it was that person you saw in the alley that night?" I looked at both Mooney and Hancock and then suddenly felt cold inside.

"What information do you have?" I asked as I brought the cig to my lips.

"Well, not much," Hancock sadly replied, "but I need to visit Mr. Vervain's house and let him know about this. I'm sure he's got no idea." I allowed the smoke of my cig to cover my worried eyes.

So that's why he's here, I thought. *That's why I saw him so frazzled after the gig. Poor guy; he's going to hate hearing about this.* "Look, I'm heading over there now. You two stay here and don't follow me." He turned and made his way for the front door, only to slowly turn around and give us a wide grin. "And seeing as how you two never listen to me, give me at least twenty minutes of a head start." He left and I couldn't decide if I wanted to laugh or just fall apart.

"Jackie," Mooney said, "you know we're going over there. Remember Dianne?"

"This is nothing like Dianne's death!" I snapped at her and then fell quiet as I sucked on my cig. I knew she was right, though.

"I know you're not angry at me," Mooney said in a calm

tone, "so I won't slap you. But yes, this is just like Dianne's death. We should have gotten her away from Sylvain sooner. In this case, we need to be there when Philippe finds out. Or, maybe he already knows and is trying to protect that family member. Whatever it is, we've got to be there." I stared at her while smoking, then handed her my car keys.

"Let's go," I replied.

—m—

W E ARRIVED AT Philippe's house exactly twenty minutes after Hancock left Mooney's house and pulled up right behind his car. We got out and looked around; no sign of either Hancock or Philippe. We then crept toward the house and up the stairs. The front door was unlocked. We glanced at each other and then slowly opened the door. Silence.

"Hancock, you here?' Monica yelled, causing me to roll my eyes.

"Well, that blew our cover," I muttered as we walked in. Suddenly, we heard a crash from the back. We raced through the house and found Hancock wrestling Philippe to the ground. I was frozen to the spot.

"Help me," Philippe screamed. "Get this dude off me!" We refused to assist; after all, Hancock was the law and we were citizens. "Alright, alright," he said while holding up his arms. "I'll be good, I promise." Hancock pulled out his handcuffs and strapped them on Philippe, then slammed him into a chair.

"Now," Hancock said while trying to catch his breath, "mind telling me why you freaked out when I showed up and why I had to chase you through your own damn house?"

Philippe hung his head against his chest and moaned, then snapped to attention and stared right at me and Monica. "He just barged in here!" he yelled. "I swear! I was minding my own business when this oaf showed up!" I could tell that Hancock wanted to deck him, so I walked up behind Hancock and placed a hand on his shoulder.

"Showed up? I told you who I was and that we needed to talk," Hancock said while still trying to calm down. "We received word that a relative of yours escaped from a mental asylum." Philippe's eyes grew wide and then began to moan. "Has this person visited you recently?" Hancock asked in a slightly pressing tone. "Son, we need to know if you've seen him. If not, then your life may be in danger. Have you seen this family member?"

Philippe stopped moaning and then began to laugh. "My life has been in danger ever since I was born," he replied while laughing. "Tainted with a dirty soul!" I cocked my head to the side; what in the world was wrong with him? He laughed so hard that he knocked the chair back and he landed on his side with a crack. He continued laughing.

"Philippe," I said as I helped him up and got him back in the chair, "talk to us, please." I glanced at Hancock, who didn't look happy that I took over in talking with him. "What do you know?" He looked deeply into my eyes and said nothing, yet there was something. I placed my hands on his shoulders and leaned in. His eyes then focused on something to the right of him. I followed his gaze and saw a small table with a box on top. Mooney, seeing the silent exchange, walked toward the table, grabbed the box, and looked inside.

"It's letters," she murmured as she pulled out a stack held together with a rubber band. "Letters."

"They never loved me," Philippe spat with a venom I'd

never heard come from him before. "Never! Always *him*, always loved him more than me! They threw me away like trash!" He struggled in the chair, yet Hancock firmly held him down while giving me a look that meant my time of talking with him was over. I moved to the side, while noticing that Philippe's eyes stayed on me. I felt like a mouse trapped by a cat.

"What are you talking about?" Hancock said, now trying to take over this mess. "Son, I'm taking you to jail to cool down."

"Fine with me, *monsieur*," Philippe replied, his glaring eyes still on me, as a thin trickle of blood fell from his nose. He raised up his handcuffed hands. "Lead the way, Napoleon!" Hancock sighed as he yanked Philippe to his feet and led him out of the house. Mooney and I watched them leave, then we too left the house and returned to my car. We placed the box of letters in the back seat and then both lit cigs. We smoked in silence for several minutes. The air was so thick with tension that you could cut it with a knife.

"Jackie," Monica said as she stared straight ahead.

"Yeah." What else could I say? What did we just witness? Had Philippe finally lost it or something?

"I think we need to return to your house and start looking," Monica replied and I slowly nodded. We drove off in silence as trails of cigarette smoke flew out of the windows.

WE ARRIVED AT my home to find Clovis working on a new piece for his trio as papers were strewn all over the living room floor. He looked up, saw us and our grim faces, and then immediately ran into the kitchen. We sat on the couch and placed the box between us. I opened the box and unfolded the first letter while Monica took the second one…

14 Avril 1933

Dear Etienne,

Bonjour! Comment ca va? It's been too long, mon amour, since we last heard from you. Surely Paris isn't that much of a distraction! I joke and I know damn well that you're loving it there. It's in our blood as Vervains, c'est pas? Your son, Philippe, is doing well; merci beaucoup for the books! Sometimes, it's so hard trying to get the perfect gift for him, especially gifted ones like our Philippe. By the way, Philippe has grown another inch! C'est fantastique! He grows like a weed, Papa says, but I can bet that it's because of our daily routines of fresh air, lots of sunshine, activity to keep him moving, and books for him to read!

As for the other . . . well, I wish you could return. He keeps asking for his Papa and I keep telling him soon. Such a shame that he's so different. I've caught him looking at the servants in the strangest manner. Just watches them conduct their daily duties around the house. I find him alone a lot. Just sitting in the library, holding a book in his hand, and staring out of the windows. I try to get him to come outside with Philippe and play, but he shakes his head no. When I try to force him (Mon Dieu!), he runs and hides from me. The only one he'll talk to is Philippe.

Tell me, Etienne, did we do something wrong? Why can't the other just be normal like Philippe? Or any little boy living in New Orleans? Sigh. Tell me what to do, Etienne. I know your art is important and it's supporting our family, but I really wish

you were here with us.
  Write soon.
  Je t'aime, toujours,
  Sylvia

I folded the letter and brought it to my nose. Lavender. I placed it to the side just as Monica finished hers. Clovis came out with a tray bearing three cups of tea. He sat on the floor and placed the tray on the middle table.

"What's going on now?" he asked as he eyed the box sitting between us. "I know that whenever Jackie gets that look, she needs tea and badly." He looked at the box and the contents. "Letters?"

"We got these from Philippe's house," I replied. "Hancock was there and he arrested him." Clovis's eyes bulged out wide like he was having a stroke.

"What?" I quickly filled him in. He shook his head in disgust. "Man," was all he said as he sipped on his tea.

"Etienne and Sylvia?" Monica asked.

"Philippe's parents," I replied, " and Sylvia is still alive, I think. She mentions another child, though. No name, just calls him 'other'." I sighed. "I had no idea Philippe had a sibling!" I wondered just what else Philippe had hidden from me and possibly others. Was he ashamed of his parents? His sibling? Is that why he didn't want to return to New Orleans?

"My letter was quite steamy between those two," Monica replied with a wolf whistle. "It was great to be French in the Thirties!"

"Those letters are from Philippe's parents?" Clovis asked. I pulled out a letter and handed it to him. He sniffed it and sighed. "Lavender," he replied as he closed his eyes, then opened them and began to read:

23 Mai 1945

Hello, my love.

Well, it's done. We just arrived home after dropping the other off. Merci beaucoup for the money. Mon Papa and Maman were there as well. Maman pleaded with me to change my mind, yet Papa agreed with me. Just like you, bien sur. I know we couldn't do anything more for the other. It's up to the doctors now. Philippe refused to come with us. Wouldn't stop crying and holding on it so tightly. I told Philippe that when we returned home, I would take him to get beignets at Cafe du Monde. He ran up to his room and locked the door.

Etienne, please, please come home. I've been wondering - do you even want to return here? To our lovely maison on St. Charles? Do you not want to see your parents again? Are you in love with someone else? I don't mind, my love. You know how I am about such matters. I know you claimed in your last letter that there was no one else, and so I believe you. Yet, please come home!

Your art is making more money than we could ever imagine! I need you. Your son needs you. We've done everything you suggested...

That...child. He was a monster! Setting fires in the house, stealing food and blaming the staff, and even pelting rocks at the birds in the trees. Whenever we caught him, he would merely smile and say in polite French that the Devil made him do it. Quelle horror! What finally did it was when I caught him painting his naked body with blood. When I asked him where he got such a vile thing, he smiled and said that Louise didn't scream at all when he cut her finger. Etienne, do you see that yes, you were right in telling us to put him away? You were right!

You left because of him, didn't you? Couldn't bear to look at his eyes.

The sun is setting and I am tired. Bon nuit, my love.

Sylvia

Clovis pinched the bridge of his nose and then read the letter out loud to Mooney and myself. We couldn't believe it. I couldn't imagine sending a child off to a hospital, even if the child was a monster as Sylvia described.

"Why do I feel like crying?" Monica asked.

"Because you would never do such a thing," I replied. "I'm sure that child wasn't as bad as they claimed, right?"

"Do people still do those kinds of things?" Clovis asked.

"I've got a friend who's a nurse at one of those kinds of places," Monica replied, "and she won't talk about what she deals with on a daily basis. I'm sure it was worse back then." I stood up to stretch my back, then chose another letter and this time read it to Clovis and Monica:

4 Decembre 1954

Philippe,

Thank you ever so much for the books and candy. I can't wait to sit back in my little room and read in silence. I always look forward to your visits, especially since no one else comes by. I miss being able to spend time with you outside of here. Thank goodness for your once a month visits and letters, of course.

I want you to know that I've stopped writing to Maman. You told me that she does read my letters but then throws them away. After all the time I spend writing, making sure that my penmanship is excellente . . . .She hates me, I know this. When you tell me the things she'd said about me, it hurts me deeply. I can't help being who and what I am. I don't care what my doctors tell me - I know I am blessed by the Devil. I'm his true son. But I digress.

How is Papa? Is he still doing well with his art? Does he ever ask about me? Does he even care? Probably not, yet one can hope. I've started painting, by the way. Just like Papa. The nurses tell me that I am quite good and they even framed one of my pieces. There is one nurse named Lucille who blushes every time she sees me. She is the one who convinced the staff to frame my work. I like talking with her, Philippe. I dream of her sometimes - thinking of her beautiful body next to mine. What would it feel like to get a kiss from her?

I'm happy for you and your continued success playing your jazz. I don't care for that type of music, preferring a good Vivaldi or perhaps some Haydn. But, we can't be completely identical, now can we? Well, I do like Armstrong. Whenever I hear him play, I wonder if he too is blessed like me. Did my true father have more than one offspring on this planet?

My eyes grew wide as I read the word *identical?*

"My god," Clovis breathed. "He's got an identical twin brother." I glanced at Monica, whose eyes were focused on the floor. I read on:

Christmas will be here soon and I am working on a new piece of art for you. I know you miss your lady friend and hopefully, this will cheer you up. I know your love for her is still strong, even after all this time of not seeing her. I know that you also love me, too. You have no idea what that means to me. You told me that you would visit me after New Years; perhaps you can come earlier? The tree will be up with all of the pretty decorations and I would love it if you could come and see it. Please let me know. I can give you your gift, rather than mail it to you.

Anyway, I hope you will write soon.

Gabriel

"Well, at least we have a name for the twin," Mooney said when I finished reading the letter. "Gabriel, son of the Devil. Twin of our friend."

"I wonder about Philippe's lady friend," I mused out loud. "Did she know about any of this?"

"Ya know," Clovis said as he lit a cig, "nothing surprises me anymore regarding Philippe." I nodded and then Mooney pulled out another letter:

3 March 1955

Philippe,

Thank you again for visiting me! When I didn't receive a reply from you, I wondered if you had received my letter at all. Quelle surprise! And those chocolates! I couldn't stop eating them after you left, and I'm afraid I got myself a little sick. But, it is normal to delve into excesses during the holidays! Lucille couldn't stop talking about you and your music, by the way. Didn't I tell you she was lovely? I've noticed, though, that she's been leaving her shift earlier than usual. Maybe she runs home to spend more time thinking about me in solitude with no worries of the other staff teasing her. I think the next time I see her, I shall declare my feelings for her. I can't offer her much, but I hope that she will take me as I am. It's all I have.

By the way, I have the most wonderful idea! I can't talk about it in this letter, for the staff reads all letters before they are sent out. Yes, I'm talking about you, Nurse Bullard! Anyway, I know you'll be coming to visit soon, so I shall tell you then. I know you'll be pleased as much as me.

Much love,
Gabriel

I looked through the remaining letters and found that this one was the most recent. I carefully placed all of the letters back in the box.

"So," Clovis said after we fell silent for a while, "now what? We know that Philippe has a twin brother named Gabriel. We know that he's been in an asylum for a long time -" Suddenly, I jumped up just as Monica snapped her fingers while her eyes went wide with surprise and understanding. "Um, am I missing something?" he asked us.

"Drive us to the police station," I yelled. Clovis grabbed his car keys and soon, we were out the door.

Once we got in the car and drove off, I explained to Clovis why Mooney and I were in shock. By the time we finished, Clovis had to hold himself back from speeding toward the station. We arrived at the police station with jittery nerves. We parked the car and raced inside, hoping like hell Hancock was around. The front desk receptionist greeted us with some reserve and told us to wait while she searched for Hancock. Clovis began to drum his fingers on the counter, while I started pacing. Monica remained unbelievably cool, yet her eyes darted from side to side.

"I'm sorry," the receptionist said, "but he left about thirty minutes ago."

"Did he tell anyone where he went?" I asked, causing her to raise an eyebrow at me.

"Are you friends of his?" she asked with a withering glance.

"Yes we are," Monica replied in her haughtiest tone, "and what we have to tell him is quite important. Now where is he?" She stared at our trio as she debated whether or not to tell us his location. Just then, I saw Officer Held reading a folder as he came around a corner. He saw me then saw Clovis and Mooney and then set his folder to the side.

"And what brings you three here?" he asked in a tone that stated he wouldn't like the answer.

"Boy, am I glad to see you," I said with relief and meant it. "Do you know where Hancock went to?"

"Yeah, he left for some house," Held replied in his thick Louisiana accent. "Claimed he got a lead." He glared at me. "You know what's going on, don't you?" He sighed and then told the receptionist that he had to escort us outside. We all walked out into the afternoon, only to stop as he placed a hand on my shoulder and turned me around. "Alright," he said, "spill."

"Look, we don't have time," I replied in a haste. "Hancock is in danger, I know it!" He looked at Monica and Clovis, who both nodded. Without another word, he led us to his patrol car and we drove to Philippe's address.

"What am I about to walk into?" he asked as he drove.

"The Devil's lair," I muttered.

WE ARRIVED AT Philippe's house and sure enough, Hancock's car was parked on the sidewalk. We jumped out of the car and raced up the stairs, noticing that the front door was open. Officer Held held up a hand, stopping us in our tracks, as he slowly drew his gun.

"Stay here," he mouthed the words and then crept into the silent house. The three of us huddled together for protection and to make sure that eyes were focused on every corner. Five minutes later, Held returned to us and told us that Hancock was downstairs. I breathed a sigh of relief as we entered the house. As we walked into the living room, I noticed a strange yet faint smell coming from the back of the house.

"Smell that?" I asked.

Mooney sniffed the air and said, "Smells like something sweet and rancid." We walked through the house and I noticed that the scent grew stronger. By the time we reached the open door leading to the basement, I wanted to throw up.

"Hancock!" Held yelled. "I've got guests."

"Sherlock and Watson, no doubt," Hancock yelled back. "Tell them to stay up there!" Held started down the stairs.

"I'm not some child to be ordered to stay put," Monica cried out as she took to the stairs, leaving Clovis and myself. I shrugged helplessly; we were already deep in it, so one more push wasn't going to make any difference. Clovis took my hand and down we went.

When we reached the bottom of the stairs, we found Hancock and Held pushing boxes away from one of the walls. I also noticed that the rancid scent was overpowering. Hancock turned to see us and grimaced.

"Damn it!" he said when he saw us. "You guys just don't listen. Help me, will ya," he said as a statement of fact. Mooney and I removed our shoes and assisted with the removal of the boxes, while Clovis pushed away smaller stacks of boxes from the wall in question.

"Dear god," I said as I stopped working and covered my mouth. "What is that?" The smell was overpowering. I could almost taste it. Hancock resumed moving boxes until he came to a section of the wall that appeared to be loosely put together. Hancock, Clovis, and Held started to remove the bricks, revealing…I screamed as Mooney fainted on the spot. Clovis threw up all over himself. Hancock rubbed his face. Held just stood there.

—◊—

MONICA'S EYES FLUTTERED open and then focused on my worried face.

"Hey," she weakly whispered, "what gives?" She looked around and noticed that she was on a rug in a sparsely furnished room. She moved into a sitting position and then looked around. "Where the hell are we?" Suddenly, images returned to her mind. She covered her mouth with her hand as tears rolled down her face.

"Where is everyone else?" she asked.

"Clovis is still here, but Held and Hancock returned to the station."

"And," she hesitated to ask, "did they . . .are they?"

"They're returning with the proper equipment to remove it," I answered while feeling sick to my stomach. *Remove it? It used to be a living human; now, it was a corpse missing a right hand. One who breathed and smiled.*

I asked Mooney if she was good and then I went outside to the front porch to smoke a cig. I needed something to calm my nerves and for a moment, I wished I had a bottle of vodka on me. However, it wouldn't do any good to be drunk while dealing with what we just discovered. I needed to be as sober as possible, because I knew that the worst had yet to come.

Several minutes later, she joined me on the front porch. We watched Ulysses Street as we smoked in silence, yet my mind was running amok. *How long had he been there? I looked around and didn't see anyone around. Did his neighbours know? Did they hear anything? I looked at Sylvain's house. Did he hear or see anything?* I shook my head. All I wanted to know was why. *Why this? Why did we find what we found? Why did he do it, if in fact he did do it? Of course he did it, I thought, but why?*

"Right now, I need a really stiff drink," Monica stated, breaking my train of black thoughts. "I don't even notice the smell that much."

"I still want to throw up," I replied. I thought about the letters again. I wanted to read all of them, if possible. Trace the entire line of how it all began in the Vervain house in New Orleans. I wanted to know more about Gabriel and Philippe. I also wanted to know if Etienne ever returned to New Orleans. I never met his parents. I remembered once that Philippe told me that his mother was not the same vibrant woman she used to be. After reading some of those letters, it was easy to see why.

"We got here too late," I stated after taking a long drag off my cig.

"Did we, Jackie?" Monica replied. "From what I've seen and read, this has been going on long before we knew Philippe." I had to agree. Several minutes later, a police car arrived and parked on the street. Hancock and Held climbed out and I was glad to see them. They carried a body bag and other accessories to help them with the terrible deed.

"Ladies," Hancock said as they walked up the front steps. Held looked grim.

Poor guy, I thought. I shouldn't have dragged him into this but then again, he would have been a part of it regardless. They walked past us and into the house. "Don't come in here at all," Hancock told us. "I'm already in serious trouble for having you three be witnesses to it all." He didn't have to worry. We saw enough.

"Clovis is inside, cleaning himself off," I said. Just then, out walked my husband, wearing only his undershirt, while his nicer shirt was tied around his waist, hiding the vomit stains. He looked embarrassed to be seen like this. He nodded to Hancock and Held and then joined us on the porch. The two cops walked in and for a moment I thought about Dante and his hellish journey.

They returned outside an hour later with the bag quite full. Monica and I moved to the side to give them room. I noticed that the smell was finally going away. We watched them load the trunk with the bag and then return to us. Held lit a cig while Hancock sat on the side. Both of their faces looked beyond shocked.

"How is he?" I asked and then regretted it. Both officers just stared at me in silence. "Stupid question, I know."

"In all of my time of being an officer of the law," Held said in a tight tone, "this is the first time I wanted to walk away from my badge."

"I used to see some strange things in New Orleans," Held offered in a voice that was barely a whisper. "The claim was that it was in the name of voodoo, but I knew better." He quickly looked away, but not before showing a very guilty face. "This . . . I just dunno."

"Did you find the severed hand?" Mooney asked, to which both cops shook their heads no. "So what now?" Mooney asked as she slowly got up and dusted herself off. "What happens to him, to us, to any of this?" She rubbed her arms as though freezing.

"What comes next will not involve you three," Hancock said with a stern warning. "I'll be talking with the trio later regarding what you know but as for now, we're taking you back to the station so you can get your car and go home." I got up with the help of Clovis and we returned to the car and drove off. Thankfully, no one wanted to say anything during the drive. I leaned my head against the window and sighed. Yeah, a stiff drink tonight. Or maybe five.

We arrived at the station and we quickly got out and into my car. Clovis drove off without any of us looking back.

"My place or yours?" I asked.

Monica shivered a bit as she crossed her arms over her chest. "Actually, drive me home. I'll see if Joan wants to have cocktails tonight. You enjoy your time with Clovis." When we pulled into the driveway some time later, she pulled me into a hug that almost cut off my breathing, kissed my cheek, and then got out of the car and almost ran into her house and locked the door. Clovis drove us home.

We walked into our home, and I immediately fell onto the couch. "I want to get roaring drunk," I told my husband. He lifted me up and hugged me so tightly that I almost couldn't breathe. *Damn it all*, I thought. *Just damn it.*

"I would join you, but I need to finish this piece." I returned to the couch, sat down, and flipped off my shoes. Clovis threw away the ruined shirt, then poured a generous amount of vodka in a glass and handed it to me. I rested my glass on top of my stomach while my eyes spotted the letter box near me. I reached for it while trying not to disturb the glass on my stomach and then set it on the floor. "Why are you going through them again, Delight?" he asked me with concern. "You know everything, right? And honestly, why do you wanna know even more of it? Let the dead stay dead."

I glared at him, but he knew I wasn't angry with him. "The dead were never dead, baby," I replied in a hot tone. "Because of what a family thought was right, someone is now dead."

"And like I said," Clovis replied, "let them stay dead. You've done your part."

"Did I?" I took a big swallow of the vodka and enjoyed the burn down my throat. "I didn't do a damn thing to save or stop any of this."

"Delight, don't beat yourself up over this. Let's face it; we couldn't have stopped any of this." Clovis stared at his feet, then slowly looked at me. "Hey . . . were you the female friend Gabriel mentioned in that letter?"

I raised my head. "What d'ya mean?"

"Maybe I'm crazy, but I think all of this involved you and you didn't even know it," Clovis replied. The wheels started spinning in my head. Was there another reason why Philippe agreed to perform in Moon City? Something he was too embarrassed, or ashamed, to tell me?

"I just need to know why," I replied as I pulled another letter out of the box and unfolded it. I took a smaller sip of my vodka and began to read:

13 February 1948

Ma cher Philippe,

I'm glad you decided to visit me here. Surely, you know why I made this choice to remain in Paris. Out of everyone there, only you have the rationale. I know that you love Gabriel but you need to understand *how much he is not your brother. That young man's mind is beyond all* understanding *to me and to your Maman. Perhaps you think I am a coward for leaving the family, but you must* understand *that I had no choice. Even though Paris is still haunted with the after effects of the War, it is still Paris. Your Maman still refused to visit me here, claiming that someone needs to keep the house going.*

Philippe, I shall be honest with you now. I hate my son, your brother. I hate him with such a passion that at times, I wonder if perhaps I could be capable of murdering him. He's no Vervain, that's for sure. That child came from the Devil himself and even though he's in an asylum, I know it will do no good. He is a monster. I remembered the day when the two of you were born. I was so proud of our growing family; here was the new generation to keep our name strong and eternal. We were one of the better families of La Nouvelle-Orleans and damn it, to have two sons meant good fortune and luck. How wrong I was.

You, in following my footsteps, have become quite the creative soul. You and your Jazz! However, I will say that it's quite popular here. Perhaps you can be part of a group here, or whatever they call them! You take after me well and for that, I am proud to call you my son. Gabriel, on the other hand, well. I am spending too much time talking about things you know. You know how intelligent he is, how charming he is. How beautiful he is. But even Lucifer himself was too beautiful to behold.

I have decided that you shall spend a month with me. I've already sent a letter to your Maman, letting her know of your journey. I'm sure she will try to talk you out of it but since Gabriel is far away, there is no reason for you to live there anymore. There, I've said it. Yes, my son, I want you to live with me. Father and son. Two artists ready to take on the world. Speaking of which, I shall be traveling to Africa to meet up with several new clients. I'll be flying to Martinique in late July. I never would have guessed that my work would be spoken of in the Dark Continent but this will be the chance of a lifetime! Perhaps you can travel with me? We shall see.

I am about to go out with my friends for dinner. Take care and I shall see you very soon.

All my love,
Etienne Vervain

I pulled my eyes away to take another sip of vodka; I could feel my body sinking into the couch. I looked down into the box and noticed a small note written on yellow paper that I had overlooked. I pulled it out of the box and began to read:

August 5, 1948

Mrs. Sylvia Vervain
New Orleans, Louisiana
We regret to inform you that Etienne Vervain has died as a result of Air France flight 072 disappearing over the Atlantic Ocean on August 1st. At this time, we have no other information, but will inform you if anything becomes apparent.

I cursed out loud, almost spilling my drink and causing Clovis to jerk his head away from this work.

"Damn it!" I yelled as I threw the note at him. He picked

it up and read it, then slowly handed it back to me. I set my drink to the side and rummaged through the box, hoping to see if he did write to his son.

"I think you've had enough of this," Clovis said as he slid the box away from me. "Get drunk and cuss me out tomorrow when you've got a raging hangover."

"No," I replied, "just one more letter. Gabriel made mention of a nurse that liked him, Lucille I think. I wonder if she was the one who was killed?"

"My wife and her gruesome ideas," Clovis said with a small laugh. "No more letters, okay? Go be a drunk and be a lush tonight." I finished off my drink and got up to refill it, then went to our bedroom with it. An hour later, I was fast asleep in bed. I didn't dream at all.

—⁂—

SEVERAL DAYS PASSED before I got a call from Hancock, ready to let me know what happened. I asked if I needed to bring Monica, to which he replied that Sherlock always needed a Watson. I smiled and then frowned as I thought about Philippe. Clovis was gone to the club for rehearsal, so I didn't have to worry about him with what I was about to do. I called Mooney after I hung up with Hancock.

"Well, give it to me straight," she said.

"Hancock wants us at the station today," I replied. "Wanna go with me?"

"Like I have a choice," she replied. "Besides, I'm your Watson. I have to know everything about this." I told her that I would pick her up in an hour and then hung up. I checked myself in the mirror several times, making sure that my already perfect look would be appropriate for a murder, and then left to pick up Monica.

When I pulled up to her house, she was standing outside waiting for me. She got into my car with a curt nod and we drove off. Neither one of us said anything, yet you could feel the tension in the air. This was going to be a horrible day for many people. We soon arrived at the police station and parked on the sidewalk. We got out of the car, and Monica immediately raced over to take my hand in hers. She gripped it tightly and said, "Ready?"

I nodded and we walked in. Hancock stood by the front desk with a cup of coffee. He saw us, nodded, and then led us through the somewhat empty station to a small room in the back. We walked in and sat down, with Hancock closing the door behind us. We stared at a dark glass panel and waited. Five minutes later, a light came on in the other room and in walked Hancock with a man in handcuffs. He gently led the man to a chair and then sat across from him, while we could see it all. The man lowered his head and took a deep breath. Hancock pulled out a pad of paper from a side drawer. I held my breath.

"State your name," Hancock said as he began to write. The man didn't move for a moment, then slowly raised his head and stared at the glass wall. "Sir," Hancock said, "please state your name for the record."

"And why," the man replied in a near whisper, "should I do that? You know who I am, don't know? Why state the obvious?"

"I know what you want me to think," Hancock replied, "so please state your full name, or else you return to your cell." The man raised up his handcuffed hands, stared at them, and then let them fall in his lap.

"My name is Philippe Michel Vervain."

"Sir, please state your name."

The man sighed. "I am Philippe Michel Vervain. Are you deaf, cop?"

"That is not your name, sir," Hancock said in an even tone. "State your name, please."

The man sighed. "My name," he said in an exaggerated Louisiana drawl, "is Philippe-" Hancock suddenly jumped out of his chair and slapped him across the face. Mooney and I glanced at each other, then returned our focus to the other room. The man hung his head low again, except now he was laughing. "Oh good one, cop," the man said as he raised his now bloody face, "hit me when I'm telling the truth."

"I know damn well you aren't telling me the truth," Hancock replied. "I'm giving you one last try, then I'm throwing you back in your cell." The man studied his handcuffed hands in silence. "Tell me your damn name!"

The man grinned as blood trickled from his nose, then he was out of his chair and rushed toward Hancock and knocked him down in a feast of strength that seemed impossible.

"Tell me *your* name!" the man laughed as he stood over Hancock. I ran out of the room and down the hall to find any cop. I located one coming out of the bathroom and told him what was going on. The cop and I then raced back to the room and I stood back as the cop rushed in, club raised, to handle the man. I returned to the other room to find Mooney biting her nails. We watched as suddenly, Philippe went docile like a kitten. He looked around the room, then at Hancock slowly getting up from the floor. "My apologies," he said like a true gentleman. "I don't know what came over me." He set the chair upright and sat down like a child ready for school. Hancock and the other cop watched him warily, then Hancock sat down again at the table.

"Let's just forget the name," Hancock stated as he nodded at the cop, who closed the door and leaned against it with arms crossed. "You know why you're here, right?"

"I'm afraid I do," Philippe replied with a sorrowful shake of his head. "Someone ran away from a lunatic asylum."

"Yes," Hancock replied in a slow tone, "and that a nurse was murdered there." He pulled out a report from the back of the pad of paper and studied it. "Lucille Jergens," he added. Philippe's eyes went wide with shock.

"Impossible!" the handcuffed man roared. "I *loved* her! She loved me!"

"According to the head doctor," Hancock went on, "she was strangled to death at the end of her shift." He glanced up at the man. "Care to tell me what you know?"

"I loved her," the man whispered repeatedly. "Just like my brother loved that colored woman, Jackie." Monica grabbed my hands as my eyes went wide. "I wanted to be like him," the man began to sob. "I told her that I loved her. I wanted to take care of her, give her books to read!"

"Well that didn't happen, now did it?" Hancock sneered. "Someone killed her before you could take her away. You wanted a normal life just like your brother, didn't you... Gabriel?" The other man stared at Hancock with eyes that looked like they were on fire. The man slowly got to his feet, just as the other cop started toward him. He stared at both men of the law then screeched, "All of you are liars!" The cop and now Hancock grabbed him by the shoulders and led him out of the room. I rushed out of the room, forgetting my safety, and faced the man I called friend in the hallway. He stopped and cocked his head as he stared at us intently.

"Get back inside!" Hancock yelled at me as the man started to resist being held by them. "This isn't a game!"

Mooney raced out and held me back. Thank goodness she was there; sometimes, it's wonderful to have a friend who's into martial arts.

"Jackie, Monica," the handcuffed man said in a now subdued voice. "It seems I'm being a rather naughty boy." He giggled and I turned away. "Tell them who I am, please! You know who I am!" Hancock and the other cop dragged him away as he continued to scream like a wild animal. Mooney and I, both stunned, returned to our room.

"What the hell is going on," Mooney muttered. "I want answers, damn it!" She paced for a moment, then stopped long enough to light a cig, then resumed pacing. I closed my eyes. I wanted answers too, especially after what we found in Philippe's house. Twenty minutes later, Hancock returned to our room and closed the door. A bruise blossomed on his left cheek, yet he looked calm and contained.

"Well, I figured that was going to go poorly," he said as he sat down in a chair across from me. "And you guys didn't help the matter. Monica, would you mind having a seat?" He held out a hand toward the empty chair.

"With all due respect, *Hancock*," she said as a stream of smoke escaped her perfect sarcastic lips, "I'll just keep pacing until you decide to fill us in on this madness!" Hancock looked at me, then Monica, and then leaned back in his chair.

"You have the letters," Hancock began in a weary tone, "and I'll need those as evidence immediately. What we're dealing with is a matter that goes back many years. You know that Philippe Vervain has a twin brother named Gabriel, correct?" We both nodded yes. "Did you know that Gabriel was sent to an asylum when he was a young man?" Mooney and I nodded yes again. "I learned that someone had escaped from the asylum some time ago and went in search of his brother. The two of them were close and Philippe was the only member of their family who actually loved him. Their artistic father, Etienne, left for Paris to continue his flourishing career. Even when the Nazis took over Paris, he was able to flee to a small town and hide in just enough time. The twins' parents loved Philippe dearly and encouraged him with his love of books and music. Gabriel, however, was treated as a stranger, an outsider, and they even went so far as to call him the Other."

"That's what we picked up in reading the letters," I stated.

Hancock nodded. "Well, once they sent Gabriel to an asylum, they thought that life would return as normal. And for a while, it did. Philippe, in being the dutiful brother, would visit Gabriel from time to time, bringing books and stories of his travels. Gabriel was and still is a monster, to be clear."

"Still is?" Monica asked as she stopped pacing.

"From the time he was born," Hancock continued, ignoring Mooney, "the family knew that Gabriel was a special child. He showed high intelligence, along with a sense of being cruel."

"Yeah," I added, "some of those letters talked about how he cut one of the servants and covered his body with the blood."

"It was more than that," Hancock replied. "He would kill small animals, torture other children, and other things." Hancock looked away for a moment, then resumed. "The family wanted nothing more to do with him, except Philippe. Philippe continued to show his twin love and caring. Even the staff commented on how much he cared for him."

"Wait a minute," I stated as a realization came to me, "one of the letters from Gabriel spoke of an idea that he couldn't wait to tell Philippe. Was his escape the great idea?"

"Yeah it was and for some strange reason, Philippe agreed with him." Hancock ran a hand through his hair. "They switched places."

"What?" Mooney and I both cried out in union.

"The twins had shown such model behaviour for a patient and visitor that the staff had begun to be lax in their viewing of them. So much so that they didn't even notice that when Philippe left the asylum, it was actually Gabriel." I began to shiver but I wasn't cold. I lit a cig with shaking fingers while Mooney repeated, "Damn," over and over. "The switch happened only recently and no one, not even his fellow jazz trio players, knew that it wasn't him."

"So what happened?" As much as I wanted to hear the rest of this kooky story, I also wanted to return home immediately.

"Philippe, now in the asylum for some time, suddenly realized that what he agreed to was horrible. He allowed his love to blind him to the fact that his twin was a monster. And now, a free monster."

"Did Gabriel ever visit Philippe?" Mooney asked.

"No," Hancock said with a sad grin. "That's when Philippe knew that he had been truly deceived. Also, he gave away his cover. According to the head doctor at the asylum, he noticed that 'Gabriel' used his right hand to write one day during their session." Hancock paused as that statement sunk in with us.

"Philippe is right handed, yeah," I said. "So what?"

"Gabriel was left handed," Hancock replied and Monica resumed pacing again. I glanced at her and knew why she resumed her pacing but decided to keep quiet. "The doctor noticed that change and asked Gabriel why he changed hands when he wrote. Of course, Philippe couldn't think of a valid reason. The doctor then quickly added that Gabriel must have been thinking of his twin brother. Philippe agreed with him. After that session, the doctor decided to keep tabs on his every move, while noticing that his brother had stopped visiting him. He also noticed that Philippe, posing as Gabriel, wasn't doing the same activities as before. When Philippe noticed that there were more nurses checking on him and deliberately calling him *Gabriel*, he knew their scheme had been found out. The final straw was when that young nurse, Lucille, discovered Philippe trying to escape. In desperation, he killed her."

My heart sank as I listened to Hancock tell us this wild and crazy tale. All that time of Philippe being here in Moon City, playing the gigs with all his might, spending time with me . . . that was Gabriel. He kept his twin brother a secret, even to me. Now, it was too late. "I'd like to see him again," I said, causing Hancock to look at me as though I'd lost my marbles.

"Are you crazy?" Mooney said behind me. "See that kook? After everything Hancock's told us, you still want to talk to him?!"

"Look," I said, trying to be reasonable, "I have to see this person one last time. I know it's crazy but I need to do it."

"Jacqueline," said Monica in a tense tone. Whenever she was worried about me, she always called me by my full name. "I want to be there with you."

I turned around in my chair and shook my head no. "This is something I need to do alone," I replied, then returned my gaze to Hancock. "Let me do this, okay?"

Hancock continued to look at me as though I needed to be locked up, but he slowly rose from his chair and made his way to the door. He opened it, walked halfway out, then turned around and said, "Well, come on, Sherlock." I got up and joined him as we made our way to the Devil's cell.

—∞—

WE WALKED DOWN the hallway that seemed to be covered in sinister shadows. Although I could hear the sounds of the other cops, I felt alone. I knew this was a dumb idea, and yet I had to look upon that face. I had to justify what I saw in that basement. Hancock kept a steady pace as we turned right and went down a flight of stairs to the cells. He never turned around once and honestly, I couldn't look at him just yet. We reached the lower level, all concrete and bars, and then turned left. Of the ten cells, only one was occupied. We walked right up to the cell's bars and then stopped to face the lonely inhabitant. He was reading *Breakfast At Tiffany's* on his narrow bed. A small pile of books sat on a table near the toilet and I noticed one of my books in that pile. He moved the book from his face, saw us, and grinned.

"Jackie," he said in that voice that I used to love, "I didn't think I would ever see you again, *cher*." He set the book down next to him, then gently patted it. "Lovely work," he murmured as his gaze fell upon the book. "So dark and yet thrilling, don't you think? Can't believe that homosexual wrote such a book, but then again…I'm lucky that Moon City has such fine bookstores." He cocked his head as the grin grew wider. "So, what brings you to my little abode? Care for some Earl Grey, or perhaps a nice Darjeeling -"

"Stop it!" I yelled as Hancock grabbed my shoulders. "Just stop it! Stop being Philippe, please!"

He placed a hand against his chest, as though my words had wounded him. "Jackie?" he asked in a truly puzzled tone. "What's wrong with you, *cher*?" He glanced at Hancock and sneered. "Never trust anyone in charge, Jackie." I grabbed the bars of the cell and lowered my head. I wanted to cry.

Hancock released my shoulders. "I think you've had enough," he said as he tried to gently pull me away, only I raised my head and stared right at him.

"Gabriel," I said coldly, causing Gabriel's face to go rigid like he'd seen a ghost. He then narrowed his eyes at me. "Gabriel Jacques Vervain," I added, "I'm not leaving until you tell me why you murdered your own twin brother and then stuffed his body behind a wall." Gabriel slowly got up from his cot and advanced toward me like a tiger about to strike. Hancock pulled me away from the bars and moved some distance back. Gabriel grabbed the bars and looked as though he could twist them like taffy.

"He was the only one who loved me," he said in a dangerously cool tone. "Not Maman and certainly not Papa. He loved me and I loved him, yet his love couldn't save me from being locked away. I felt like an animal at that asylum. All those tests! They . . hurt." He lowered his head and it sounded like he was growling. "I told my brother about those tests," he moaned, "yet he couldn't do anything about it. Always leaving me there while he went to live his glamorous life. Lucille…was the light in that place of darkness. Seeing her smile for me and me alone made me have hope. It was her who kept my spirit alive. She loved my artwork and got it framed. I hated it when she would leave for the day. Even when I found out that she had someone in her life, I knew that he couldn't give her what I could. So, I came up with the bright idea to switch places with my brother!"

"But he loved playing jazz and traveling," I replied in disbelief. "The last time we talked, he told me how much he enjoyed his life on the road. I just can't believe it and now, I can't even ask him if it's true."

"He always brought your letters to me to read," Gabriel said sadly and I almost believed his sorrow. "He missed you and yes, he loved you. When your husband invited us to perform here, I knew that I couldn't refuse! A chance to finally meet the infamous Jacqueline Verona! But, I'm going ahead of myself." He crossed his legs as though we were enjoying dinner at a restaurant. "When I told him of my idea, that fool actually wanted to help me! He knew that I never had a chance to enjoy the world and so sacrificed his freedom for mine." He raised his head up and I noticed that there were tears on his face.

"Jackie," Hancock told me as he tried to push me away, "you've heard enough. Let's go upstairs." I shrugged him off, causing Gabriel to smile at me again.

"Yes," he purred at me, "you *do* want to know, don't you? We switched places on a rainy Monday. Rather easy. We were the model patient and visitor for so long. They knew we could do no wrong. So, they didn't think anything of it when I walked out wearing my brother's snazzy clothes, while he donned my white pajamas. I walked out to freedom and no one was the wiser!"

"But why did you murder him?" said a voice behind us. I turned to see Monica walking toward us and I was actually grateful to see her. "Why kill the one man who helped and loved you?"

"Ah," he said as he turned his gaze toward Mooney, "the lesbian! Do you know, I saw so many of your *kind*," he spat out, "in there? And they thought I was horrific! But," Gabriel said with a small bow, "I digress. The woman lover wants to know why I murdered my twin brother? Simple - he was going to rat me out *and* he killed Lucille! He escaped the asylum after murdering that beautiful flower and hunted me down. Me, the wildly successful jazz sax player! He met up with me at one gig in Chicago and I was shocked! I took him in, of course. After a while, he asked why I never visited him. I replied that I no longer needed his protection. I had the life I'd always wanted - *his*."

I stared at him in shock.

"Yes," he said as he slowly nodded, "you're getting it, aren't you. I never loved my brother, while he actually loved me. I used my dear Philippe! When he found out, well, he blew his lid. Told me that he was going to tell the 'fuzz' about our little swap. I quickly left town, yet he followed me like a dog.

"When I arrived in Moon City, I knew he was going to come here. He talked about you so much that I, too, began to fall in love with you. That night of the gig, Philippe wanted to talk with me in the alley and yes, I saw you watching us. He was going on and on again about telling the fuzz and he also wanted to tell you too. I yelled out 'No' and that I would help him instead. I told him that we would switch back our identities and no one would know. He then told me about Lucille. What he'd done to her. He said that I had no choice in helping him. I acted as though he was right. I told him to meet up with me after the gig, and I killed him." He rubbed his hands together with such malicious glee. "The look in his eyes when I struck the first blow - glorious. He didn't cry out, actually. Maybe he knew it would eventually come to this. Once I killed him, I needed a place to hide his body. I didn't want to do the cliche act of throwing him into a river or a lake."

"So you shoved his body into a part of the basement wall," Mooney finished for him, "in your brand new house you bought as you claimed you were looking for a fresh start."

"And I was," Gabriel replied. "I wanted to get everything ready for Lucille. I wanted to marry her and grow old with her. I also wanted Philippe to have a home here as well," he added. "I was working on a plan to get you away from your husband and to finally be reunited with Philippe." Gabriel started to rock back and forth. "It was going to be perfect, until that idiot threatened me and killed my love." He rocked faster. "Perfect, perfect, perfect," he said in a singsong voice.

"One thing that puzzles me," I asked, fearing the answer, "why was Philippe's right hand cut off?"

Gabriel laughed, sounding as though we were all just spending time at someone's house and not in the jail area of a police station. "I figured you would pick up on that," he replied. "*C'est simple* - he was right handed. It was a memento for me. Don't bother looking for it," he finished as he rubbed his belly and made smacking noises.

Monica turned me away from that monster and led me upstairs, as Hancock stayed behind. I refused to say anything until I reached the car. We held each other tightly as we walked through the station. All eyes were on us. They knew. We walked outside into the beautiful sunny day and toward my car. We got in, immediately lit cigs, and then I started to cry. No, I didn't cry. I bawled. Mooney got out of the car and opened my door, then pulled me out and changed places with me. She drove us to her house while I continued to wail for my dead friend.

—⁂—

For weeks, I couldn't write but instead slept off and on, smoked too much, and drank enough tea to float the entire city. Hancock called me several days after my meeting with Gabriel to inform me that he had been returned to the asylum and placed under maximum supervision. There was also talk of a lobotomy but I never found out if it happened. Honestly, I didn't care. I wanted my friend back.

Clovis found out everything through Mooney and he went from super busy to super protective of me. I knew he was worried about his Delight suddenly cracking up and being shipped off to the loony farm like Gabriel. He was also concerned that a so-called friend of mine and his kooky twin brother were crazy in love with me. Yet, even though I barely talked to him, I wasn't going crackers. Monica, my best and dearest friend, contacted Jean and Leon in New Orleans and told them of the news. From what she told me, they couldn't believe it. They had been touring with Gabriel for years and never knew that it wasn't Philippe. He acted, as I had to agree with them, so much like Philippe.

There was a jazz funeral for Philippe with a closed casket, of course. Thousands flocked to New Orleans to pay their respects for the once beloved sax player. The coffin was buried in the family plot and soon became a shrine for all jazz lovers and those who loved Philippe.

As much as I didn't want to attend the funeral, I knew I had to. So, Clovis, Monica, and I drove to New Orleans to say goodbye. The only family members that showed up were several cousins and the twins' mother, now old and frail. She was in a wheelchair and was dressed in her finest black, yet her eyes still showed some of the fire Philippe used to talk about. Although I wanted to stay hidden from the family, they soon saw me and descended upon me with kisses as though I was part of the family.

—m—

WHEN WE RETURNED to Moon City, Monica informed me that she was going to spend some alone time with Joan and to not worry about her. I knew she needed it, considering everything we'd gone through. I left her alone and returned to my typewriter and intimate time with Clovis. Three days later, I got a phone call from Mooney and, gosh darn it, the kid was head over heels in love.

"I'm tellin' ya," she said in a dreamy tone, "Joan sets me on fire!" She giggled a little and it made my soul feel good to hear my friend be herself again.

"I'm truly happy for you," I replied.

"Jackie...I told her everything," she said. "I wanted her to know why I'd been quiet for a while. She understood. Said it reminded her of her time with that guy, Charlie. Gruesome."

"Yeah. Well you two'll have to come by for drinks one night," I offered.

Monica went quiet and then said, "Sure about that? I mean, with what happened..."

"Look, my friend is now in the ground. His crazy brother is locked away for good. As much as I miss that crazy bastard, I need to go on, ya know? And that includes spending time with my best friend and her new love, while all four of us get plastered."

"Sounds good and I'll bring appetizers!" We hung up and I touched my face. Yes, I was smiling. I touched my face again and felt the tears streaming down my face. *Crazy, crazy bastard*, I thought.

THE NEXT DAY, Clovis walked into my office to find me furiously typing on my typewriter. He leaned against the door frame and watched me in silence and with relief. I stopped when I heard him cough; I turned around and gave him a shaky smile.

"You alright, Delight?" I nodded yes. He smiled back, then reached in his back pocket to pull out a small letter and then left. I felt myself go cold when I saw the return address. With shaking hands, I tore open the envelope and unfolded the letter, as the barest hint of lavender came from the letter:

Jackie,

May I call you that, or would you prefer Jacqueline? I guess I am the last person you want to hear from, no? Before you spit upon this letter and then bury it, let me tell you this: it was truly a pleasure meeting you as myself. You are quite lovely for a coloured woman. Intelligent too. I have access to all of your books here and I've been devouring them like crazy. Talented but then again, my brother never spent time with anyone who was inferior. We had that in common. I have a gift for you, Jacqueline. In fact, you should receive it very soon. Do write back and let me know what you think of it. I painted it with you in mind.

And now, I must say au bientot, for they are coming around with the nightly medicine. Soon, I will be fast asleep, hopefully dreaming of you and your beauty. Know that I am always thinking of you, my dearest Jacqueline. Know that I am always watching you.

I am yours forever,
Gabriel

I tore the letter to pieces and rushed into the kitchen to burn it, when I heard a knock at the door. I returned to the living room to find Clovis accepting a medium sized package from a delivery man, then closing the door. He studied the package for a moment and then handed it to me.

"I'm sure that letter was nothing good," he said as I walked over to the couch with the package in my hands and sat down. The kraft paper wrapped package felt quite light; I unwrapped it slowly while Clovis watched with anticipation. When the last of the paper fell away, I held out the painting and stared at it for a very long time. The painting depicted a beautiful coloured woman dressed in a flowing red dress, while a sinister figure, dressed in black and with bright blue eyes, stood behind her. He held a rose in front of her in a gloved left hand, while his right hand had not been painted in. The woman looked just like me, while the man looked just like Gabriel.

"Give it to me and I'll trash it," Clovis said as he took the painting from me, yet I took it from him and cradled it to my chest. "Hey, what gives?" he asked. "You got a thing for loony men now?"

I said nothing, yet got up and returned to my office, closing the door behind me. I set the painting on top of a small table against a wall, then sat in my chair and studied it for a very long time. As much as I wanted to forget that monster, I knew that I couldn't. I also knew, as I lit a cig and blew smoke at the painting, that I would see Gabriel Jacques Vervain again.

And that next time, I would be ready.

The End

ABOUT THE AUTHOR

KIMBERLY B. RICHARDSON is the author of multiple novels and anthology stories. Ms. Richardson was the 2015 David McCrosky Volunteer Photographer in Residence for Elmwood Cemetery in Memphis, Tennessee. Her photography was featured in the New Orleans Photo Alliance 2020 exhibition What is French in Louisiana. She is the founder and owner of Viridian Tea Company and a World Tea Academy Certified Tea Specialist. She resides in Colorado.

Made in the USA
Columbia, SC
25 April 2022

59415515R00054